THE TIME GATE

Mystery of the Lost City

© copyright page

Except as permitted by copyright law applicable to you, you may not reproduce or transmit any content on this book, without the permission of the copyright owner.

Australian copyright law allows certain uses of content from the Internet without the copyright owner's permission. This includes uses by educational institutions, Commonwealth and state governments, provided fair compensation is paid. For more information see www.copyright.com.au and www.copyright.org.au.

Owners of copyright in content on this Book may receive compensation for the use of their content by educational institutions and governments, including from licensing schemes operated by the copyright agency.

© 2025, PonPon

TABLE OF CONTENTS

INTRODUCTION 4

THE DISCOVERY 14

THE TIME GATE 28

MEETING THE PRINCESS 47

THE LOST CITY'S SECRET 66

THE TYRANT KING 86

ESCAPE AND PURSUIT 105

A JOURNEY FOR HOPE 125

THE KEY TO TIME 144

BETRAYAL 163

THE FINAL BATTLE 181

RESTORING BALANCE 199

BACK TO THE PRESENT 217

INTRODUCTION

Ethan Carter had always been fascinated by the past. While other kids spent their weekends playing video games or watching movies, he found himself wandering through antique shops, running his fingers over old books, dusty globes, and faded photographs of people long forgotten. There was something about history that made him feel alive, as if every object from the past held a secret waiting to be uncovered.

It was on one of these ordinary Saturday afternoons that Ethan stumbled upon something extraordinary. The small antique shop at the corner of Brookdale Street was a place he had visited a dozen times before, but this time, something was different. As he browsed through a shelf filled with vintage pocket watches, one particular watch caught his eye.

It was old—far older than anything else in the store. The metal casing was tarnished, yet the intricate engravings on its surface shimmered faintly under the dim shop lights. Strange symbols covered the back, ones Ethan had never seen before. When he picked it up, an odd sensation coursed through him, like a jolt of static electricity.

"Ah, you have a good eye," came a voice from behind the counter.

Ethan turned to see the shop's owner, Mr. Whitaker, a frail old man with piercing gray eyes. He smiled, though there was something unreadable in his expression.

"This watch," Ethan said, running his fingers over the cool metal. "It feels... different."

Mr. Whitaker chuckled, but it wasn't a warm laugh. It was more knowing—almost as if he expected Ethan to say that. "That piece has been in my collection for a long time," he said. "No one ever showed much interest in it. But if you listen closely, it has a story to tell."

Ethan held the watch up to his ear. To his surprise, he didn't hear the steady ticking of a clock. Instead, there was a faint hum, a whisper-like sound that seemed to shift and change, as if a voice were trapped inside.

"How much?" Ethan asked, his curiosity fully awakened.

Mr. Whitaker hesitated for just a moment before naming a price. It wasn't expensive—almost as if the shopkeeper wanted him to take it. Without thinking twice, Ethan handed over the cash, tucked the watch into his pocket, and left the store, unaware that his life had just changed forever.

That night, as Ethan lay in bed, he couldn't shake the strange feeling the watch gave him. He turned it over in his hands, tracing the strange engravings. Then, just as he pressed the small button on its side—

A blinding light filled his room.

The air around him crackled with energy, and before he could even let out a scream, the world around him dissolved. The walls of his bedroom faded into darkness, and he felt himself being pulled—through time, through space, through something he couldn't comprehend.

And when the light finally cleared, Ethan found himself standing in a place he had never seen before.

A massive city stretched before him, its golden towers gleaming under an unfamiliar sun. People in flowing robes and armor moved through the streets, their voices echoing in a language he didn't recognize. The scent of spices and burning torches filled the air.

But before he could take another step, a voice rang out.

"Seize him!"

Ethan barely had time to react before rough hands grabbed his arms, pulling him forward. A group of armored guards surrounded him, their eyes filled with suspicion.

"Where am I?" he gasped, struggling against their grip.

"You will answer to King Darius," one of the guards growled.

And just like that, Ethan realized he was no longer in his own time.

He had stepped into the past—a past that wasn't supposed to exist.

Ethan's heart pounded against his ribs as the guards dragged him through the narrow streets. His mind raced, trying to make sense of what had just happened. A moment ago, he had been in his bedroom, staring at an old pocket watch. Now, he was somewhere else—somewhen else.

The city around him was unlike anything he had ever seen before. Towering structures of polished stone rose high into the sky, adorned with glowing symbols that pulsed like embers in the wind. The streets were paved with smooth, golden tiles, and merchants in elaborate robes called out from market stalls, selling fruits Ethan had never seen, fabrics woven with silver threads, and gleaming trinkets that seemed to hum with energy. The people walked with purpose, their eyes sharp, their faces determined. There was something about this place—something ancient yet impossibly advanced, as if time itself had folded in strange and mysterious ways.

But Ethan had no time to take it all in.

The guards, clad in dark armor engraved with swirling patterns, pulled him forward with iron grips. Their expressions were unreadable, their steps heavy against the golden pavement. Ethan struggled, but their strength was overwhelming.

"Wait! There's been a mistake!" he gasped, his voice barely above a whisper. "I don't belong here!"

The leader of the guards, a tall man with a jagged scar across his cheek, turned to him with narrowed eyes. "You wear the mark of the Watch," he said, nodding toward Ethan's clenched fist.

Ethan looked down and realized he was still gripping the pocket watch tightly. The strange engravings on its surface glowed faintly, as if responding to something unseen.

"What does that mean?" Ethan demanded.

The guard ignored him, turning back toward the massive palace that loomed ahead.

Ethan's breath hitched. The palace was an architectural wonder—colossal gates of bronze stood open, revealing an inner courtyard filled with towering pillars, cascading waterfalls, and floating lanterns that bobbed in the air like fireflies. The building itself was carved into a mountainside, with grand staircases winding upward, disappearing into shadowy halls.

At the heart of it all, seated on an elaborate throne of obsidian and gold, was a man Ethan knew instinctively was the king.

King Darius.

His presence was overwhelming. He was tall and broad-shouldered, his dark robes lined with shimmering silver that seemed to move like liquid metal. His face was strong, with sharp cheekbones and piercing golden eyes that glowed faintly in the dim light. A heavy crown, adorned with a single, glowing gemstone, rested upon his head. He exuded power—an aura of command that made the air feel heavier around him.

The guards forced Ethan to his knees before the throne.

Silence filled the grand hall. The tension in the air was suffocating.

King Darius leaned forward, studying Ethan with a gaze so intense it felt like it could strip away every secret he had. "You are not of this world," he said at last, his voice deep and controlled. "And yet, you wear the Watch."

Ethan swallowed hard. He had no idea how to respond.

Darius rose from his throne, his robes flowing like liquid shadow. He stepped down from the platform, moving closer, his eyes never leaving Ethan's. "Do you even know what you hold?"

Ethan hesitated, then shook his head. "I found it in an antique shop… I didn't know it would bring me here."

Darius let out a quiet chuckle, but there was no humor in it. "It did not bring you here, boy. It chose you."

Ethan's grip tightened around the watch. "Chose me for what?"

The king tilted his head slightly, as if considering something. "That remains to be seen."

Then, without warning, he raised a hand. The air shimmered. A gust of energy surged through the room, crackling with power. Ethan felt an invisible force wrap around him, lifting him off the ground.

He struggled, but his limbs were paralyzed. The watch in his hand vibrated wildly, glowing brighter and brighter.

And then, just as quickly as it had begun, the energy dissipated, and Ethan collapsed back onto the cold floor, gasping for breath.

Darius smiled—calm, calculating. "Yes… you may be useful after all."

Before Ethan could react, the king turned to the guards. "Take him to the Tower. He is not to leave until I say otherwise."

The guards seized Ethan once more, dragging him back through the grand hall.

Panic set in.

He had no idea where he was. No idea how to get back home.

And worst of all—he wasn't sure he wanted to leave.

Because for the first time in his life, Ethan Carter had stepped into a mystery far bigger than anything he had ever imagined.

And something deep inside him told him that this was just the beginning.

THE DISCOVERY

The dusty air of the old antique shop was thick with the scent of aged wood, faded paper, and something else—something Ethan couldn't quite place. It smelled like history, like forgotten stories trapped between the cracks of ancient furniture and the brittle pages of books no one had touched in decades. The shop was dimly lit, the golden glow of a single flickering lantern casting long shadows over the shelves that loomed above him.

Ethan Carter had never been the type to wander into places like this. He wasn't one to admire old trinkets or imagine the past lives of objects long discarded. But today was different. Today, something had pulled him in, an unseen force whispering in the back of his mind, urging him to step inside.

He ran his fingers over a dusty oak table covered with all sorts of strange objects—rusty keys, delicate porcelain figurines, ornate daggers with gemstones embedded in their hilts. But none of it interested him. He had almost turned to leave when something in the corner of the shop caught his eye.

A small wooden box sat on a velvet cloth, its surface darkened with age. The lid was slightly ajar, revealing a glint of something metallic inside.

Drawn by an inexplicable curiosity, Ethan reached for it. The wood was smooth, almost warm to the touch, as if it had been waiting for him. Slowly, he lifted the lid.

Inside, nestled in black satin, was a pocket watch.

It was unlike any he had ever seen. Its casing was silver, but not like normal silver—this metal seemed to pulse faintly, as though it were alive, shifting under the dim light. The face was intricate, covered in swirling engravings that twisted in mesmerizing patterns. There were no numbers, only strange symbols etched around the edges, symbols that seemed to shimmer when he looked at them from different angles.

Ethan felt a strange pull in his chest. He reached out, hesitating only for a moment before his fingers closed around the watch.

The instant he touched it, a jolt of energy shot up his arm.

It wasn't painful, but it was powerful. A tingling sensation spread through his fingertips, up to his wrist, and then further, seeping into his bones like an electric current humming beneath his skin. His vision blurred for a fraction of a second, and in that brief moment, he swore he saw something—images flashing across his mind like fragments of a forgotten dream. A city bathed in golden light. A tower stretching toward a storm-filled sky. A figure cloaked in shadows, eyes burning like molten gold.

Then, just as quickly as it had come, the sensation faded.

Ethan staggered back, his breath shallow. The shop around him seemed unchanged, the dust still clinging to the air, the shelves still lined with forgotten relics. But something had shifted. Something inside him.

"What… was that?" he muttered under his breath, his grip tightening around the watch.

"You felt it, didn't you?"

Ethan spun around.

Behind the counter stood an old man, his face lined with deep wrinkles, his eyes dark and knowing. He had been there the whole time, yet Ethan had barely noticed him before now.

"I—" Ethan hesitated. "I don't know what just happened."

The old man stepped closer, his gaze falling to the watch in Ethan's hand. "It's been a long time since anyone has touched that," he said, his voice low, almost reverent. "And even longer since it chose someone."

"Chose?" Ethan repeated, his pulse quickening. "What do you mean?"

The old man studied him carefully before shaking his head. "That's not for me to say." He nodded toward the watch. "But if you can feel its power… then your journey has already begun."

Ethan swallowed hard.

Something inside him told him that this was no ordinary watch. That it was far older, far more important than it appeared. And that, somehow, his life had just changed forever.

But what that meant... he had no idea.

Ethan's fingers curled around the watch, its cold metal sending another shiver through his palm. The weight of it felt oddly significant—heavier than it should be, as though it carried something unseen within its casing. His pulse thudded in his ears as he turned it over, tracing the strange engravings with his thumb. The symbols weren't random. They looked almost... intentional, like an ancient language whispering a forgotten truth.

The old man behind the counter watched him carefully, his lined face unreadable.

"You should put it back," he murmured, his voice a raspy warning.

Ethan hesitated. His instinct told him to listen, to heed the caution in the man's tone. But there was another feeling, a deeper pull—like the watch wanted him to hold it, like it had been waiting for him.

"What is this?" Ethan asked, his voice barely above a whisper.

The old man sighed, rubbing a gnarled hand over his chin. "That's a question with many answers, boy. But none of them will make sense to you just yet."

The response only fueled Ethan's curiosity. He turned the watch over again, his eyes narrowing as he noticed a small latch on its side. It was barely visible, blended into the swirling designs, but now that he saw it, he couldn't ignore it.

Without thinking, he pressed it.

Click.

The watch face popped open.

Ethan expected to see the delicate gears of a normal pocket watch, the intricate workings of timekeeping mechanisms. But what lay inside was nothing ordinary.

A thin, swirling mist curled from the watch's interior, tendrils of silver and blue unfurling like living smoke. It moved unnaturally, spiraling upward before dispersing into the air. Ethan's breath caught in his throat as the symbols on the watch's face pulsed—one by one, they lit up, glowing faintly before fading back to their original form.

Then, without warning, a deep, resonant chime echoed through the shop.

The sound wasn't just heard—it was felt, vibrating through Ethan's bones like an invisible wave crashing over him. The lights flickered. The air itself seemed to tremble.

And then… a voice.

It wasn't the old man's voice. It wasn't his own.

It was something else.

A whisper, low and ancient, curling through the shop like a breeze that carried forgotten secrets.

"Time bends for those who dare to hold its weight."

Ethan stumbled back, his breath shallow. His fingers trembled, but he couldn't bring himself to let go of the watch.

"What the hell was that?" he gasped.

The old man's face had gone pale, his lips pressed into a thin line. He took a slow, deliberate step forward, eyes locked onto the watch as though it might strike at any moment.

"You need to leave," he said.

Ethan blinked. "What?"

"Take the watch. Go." The man's voice was urgent now, edged with something close to fear. "You've woken it. And that means... you don't have much time."

The words sent a chill down Ethan's spine. He wanted to ask more, to demand an explanation, but something in the old man's gaze stopped him. This wasn't a joke. This wasn't just some eerie trinket.

Something had truly awakened.

Swallowing hard, Ethan shoved the watch into his pocket. The metal burned cold against his skin, but he ignored it. Without another word, he turned and pushed open the shop door, stepping out into the cold night air.

The door swung shut behind him with a hollow *thud*.

For a moment, the world outside felt... normal. The street was quiet, the glow of streetlamps casting golden pools of light onto the pavement. Cars rumbled in the distance. A couple passed by, laughing softly, oblivious to the strange energy still thrumming through Ethan's veins.

But something was different.

The air felt heavier. The stars above seemed sharper, too bright, as if they were watching him. And in the far distance, beyond the city skyline, dark clouds were gathering—swirling unnaturally, spiraling inward toward a single unseen point.

Ethan exhaled slowly, his breath curling in the cold night air.

He had a feeling that whatever had just begun…

It wasn't going to stop.

Ethan stood frozen on the sidewalk, his breath unsteady as the city hummed around him. The weight of the pocket watch in his palm felt heavier than before, as if something unseen had shifted inside it. He could still feel the echo of that voice— low, ancient, filled with something beyond his understanding.

"Time bends for those who dare to hold its weight."

What did that even mean?

The night air pressed against his skin, colder than it had been just moments ago. A sharp gust of wind whistled down the street, rattling signs and sending a loose newspaper skittering across the pavement. Ethan's instincts screamed at him to throw the watch away, to get rid of it, but his fingers refused to release their grip.

He glanced back at the antique shop, half-expecting to see the old man watching him from the window. But the store was dark now. The neon "Open" sign had flickered off. Had the man shut it down the moment he left?

Ethan's stomach twisted.

Something was wrong.

Shaking his head, he stuffed the watch into his jacket pocket and started walking. The streets of downtown Boston were mostly empty this late at night, save for the occasional car rolling by. Streetlights flickered above him, their glow dimmer than usual, casting elongated shadows along the sidewalk.

He turned a corner, heading toward the subway station. The rhythmic *tap tap* of his footsteps echoed in the quiet. Normally, the sound was familiar, comforting. Tonight, it felt like something was following him.

Ethan glanced over his shoulder. Nothing.

Still, that unease didn't leave him. If anything, it deepened.

He pulled his jacket tighter around himself and quickened his pace. The entrance to the subway was just ahead, its concrete steps leading down into the dimly lit underground. A lone street musician played a slow, haunting tune on his violin near the entrance, the melody carrying through the still air.

Ethan descended the stairs, his heart pounding. The station was nearly empty—just a couple of people waiting on the platform, staring at their phones. A low hum filled the air, the ever-present buzz of subway lights mixed with the distant rumble of an approaching train.

He leaned against a pillar, trying to steady his breathing.

"It's just a watch," he told himself. *"A weird, creepy watch. That's all."*

But he didn't believe it.

The memory of the mist, the symbols, the voice—it all felt too real. And then there was the old man's warning. *You don't have much time.* What had he meant? Was something coming for him?

A rush of cold air swept through the station. The train was arriving.

The moment the metal beast roared into the platform, Ethan felt a strange sensation in his chest—like something was pulling at him, a deep gravitational force tugging at his core. The lights flickered as the subway doors slid open with a hiss.

He stumbled forward, his vision swimming. The world tilted.

And then, for just a second—barely a blink—everything changed.

The station around him flickered. The people vanished. The modern subway car was replaced by something else—something older. The walls of the station looked different, worn, like they belonged to a century long past. The train itself was no longer sleek metal but a dark, iron locomotive, its windows glowing with dim candlelight. The air smelled of smoke and aged paper.

Ethan gasped.

Then—just as quickly as it had come—the vision snapped away.

The subway station returned to normal. The people were back, staring at their phones. The train was just an ordinary train, its fluorescent lights buzzing softly.

Ethan stood there, breathless, his fingers digging into his jacket pocket. He felt the watch pulsing, a rhythmic, steady beat against his palm—like the ticking of a heart.

He staggered backward, his mind racing.

He wasn't imagining this.

Something was happening.

Something real.

The subway doors beeped, signaling their imminent closure. Without thinking, Ethan turned and sprinted up the stairs, ignoring the curious glances from a few late-night commuters. He burst back onto the city streets, sucking in gulps of cool air.

His hands shook as he pulled out the watch and stared at it. The symbols were still faintly glowing, the metal unnaturally warm.

Ethan swallowed hard.

This wasn't just an old antique.

This watch—whatever it was—had *power*.

And now, it belonged to him.

THE TIME GATE

The night air was thick with an eerie silence as Ethan sprinted down the empty streets, his heart pounding in his chest. The pocket watch burned against his palm, radiating a warmth that felt unnatural. The vision—the flickering glimpse of another era—still haunted his mind. He had seen something impossible. Something real.

His breath came in ragged gasps as he turned down an alleyway, leaning against a cold brick wall. The city around him felt different now, like a thin veil had been lifted, revealing cracks in reality. He could still hear the train's whistle echoing in his mind—not the sleek subway's mechanical chime, but the deep, mournful cry of an old steam locomotive.

"What the hell is happening?" he muttered, his fingers tightening around the watch.

He had to figure this out.

Ethan exhaled sharply, forcing himself to focus. He flipped the pocket watch open, its face glowing faintly in the darkness. The symbols inside pulsed, shifting in patterns that seemed to respond to his presence. His fingers traced the delicate engravings, searching for anything that might explain what was happening.

Then he noticed it.

The small latch—the same one he had pressed before—had changed. Now, it was glowing. Almost... beckoning.

He hesitated. Last time he pressed it, something *woke up*. Something powerful.

But he had to know.

Slowly, he pressed the latch.

Click.

A low hum filled the air.

The pocket watch vibrated against his palm, and the symbols flared to life, burning brighter than before. A thin tendril of blue mist seeped from the watch's interior, curling in the air like smoke. Ethan's pulse quickened as the mist began to swirl faster, coiling around his hand, then his arm, until his entire body was engulfed in shimmering light.

The alleyway around him blurred, the brick walls warping, bending, dissolving into streaks of golden energy. His feet left the ground. He felt weightless, as if reality itself had lost its grip on him. The city faded. The sounds of traffic, distant sirens, and streetlights buzzing—all of it melted away.

Then—silence.

A cold rush of air struck his skin.

Ethan landed hard, his knees buckling beneath him. He gasped, inhaling air that was thick with the scent of something unfamiliar—earthy, metallic, tinged with the faintest hint of burning wood. His fingers dug into dirt, not concrete.

He slowly lifted his head.

And what he saw stole the breath from his lungs.

He was no longer in Boston.

Towering stone buildings rose around him, their surfaces worn with time yet grand and imposing. The structures were unlike anything he had ever seen—massive columns lined the streets, carved with intricate symbols, eerily similar to the ones on the pocket watch. The architecture was ancient, yet impossibly advanced, a strange blend of forgotten history and something beyond human comprehension.

Ethan stumbled to his feet, his eyes darting around. The sky above him was vast, tinged with hues of deep gold and twilight blue, with twin suns hovering on the horizon. The air felt charged, humming with unseen energy.

Then, he heard them.

Voices.

He turned sharply. Down the massive stone road, figures were approaching—tall, robed figures, their faces obscured by ornate metallic masks. They moved with purpose, their flowing garments shimmering in the soft light. In their hands, they carried staffs tipped with glowing crystals, pulsing with an energy that made Ethan's skin tingle.

Panic surged through him.

"Where the hell am I?"

He took a step back, but his foot hit something solid. He whirled around—behind him stood a massive archway, carved from dark stone. Strange symbols pulsed along its surface, forming a perfect circle. The energy within the arch swirled like liquid gold, rippling outward in waves.

The *gate*.

His heart pounded. Had the watch transported him through *time?*

The robed figures were closer now. Their voices were low, their language unfamiliar, yet strangely melodic. One of them raised a hand, motioning toward Ethan.

The pocket watch in his hand vibrated violently.

And then, without warning, the archway behind him let out a deep, resonant *boom*.

The air around it cracked, as if reality itself was splitting open. The golden energy within the arch shimmered, then pulsed outward in a shockwave. Ethan barely had time to react before a surge of light engulfed him once more.

And then—darkness.

Ethan's body felt weightless, as though he were drifting between worlds. His vision swam with shifting colors—gold, blue, and deep crimson—melding together in an endless void. A strange pressure surrounded him, as if time itself was holding its breath. The sensation was neither painful nor pleasant, but utterly alien, like standing at the edge of existence.

His heartbeat pounded in his ears.

Then—impact.

The world snapped back into focus with a force that sent Ethan sprawling onto the ground. He hit the earth hard, the breath knocked from his lungs. He coughed, his fingers clawing at the ground beneath him. It wasn't concrete. It wasn't asphalt. It was rough, uneven stone, warm beneath his touch as if it had been baking under the sun.

A sharp, dry wind swept over him, carrying the scent of ancient dust and something metallic, like rusted iron. Ethan groaned and forced himself onto his hands and knees. His entire body ached from the fall, but nothing seemed broken. His fingers instinctively clenched around the pocket watch, its surface still warm, still humming with the strange energy that had brought him here.

Here.

The realization hit him like a freight train.

He wasn't in Boston.

He wasn't *anywhere* he recognized.

He lifted his head. The world around him was… impossible.

Towering structures of weathered stone stretched into the sky, their surfaces etched with intricate carvings—symbols that mirrored those inside the pocket watch. The streets beneath him were paved with massive slabs of smooth, dark rock, forming a pathway that stretched in both directions. Beyond the towering structures, the sky was a canvas of deep violet and gold, with not one, but two suns casting an eerie glow over the city.

Ethan staggered to his feet, his head still spinning.

"This… this can't be real."

But it *was* real.

Every breath he took filled his lungs with warm, dry air. Every sound—the distant murmur of voices, the whisper of the wind against stone—was vivid and tangible. He wasn't dreaming. He wasn't hallucinating.

He had traveled through time.

A surge of panic twisted in his gut. *How do I get back?*

The pocket watch.

His fingers fumbled to open it again. He flipped the lid, expecting to see the same glowing symbols, the same hum of energy that had swallowed him before. But the watch was different now. The hands were frozen, unmoving. The pulsing glow had dimmed, as if whatever force had powered it was… dormant.

Ethan swallowed hard.

No. No, no, no.

His chest tightened. He pressed the latch again. Nothing. He shook it. Nothing. The watch, the *one thing* that had brought him here, was suddenly silent.

"Damn it!"

His voice echoed through the empty street. The only answer was the whisper of the wind.

Then—footsteps.

Ethan froze.

They were soft at first, barely audible, but growing louder, more deliberate. Someone was approaching. He turned slowly, his pulse hammering against his ribs.

Down the street, moving toward him with slow, measured steps, was a group of figures.

They wore long, flowing robes of deep crimson and gold, their hoods pulled low over their faces. At first, they almost looked human—but as they neared, Ethan's breath caught in his throat. Their faces were obscured by metallic masks, intricately designed with swirling engravings. Some had elongated, curved designs, while others were smooth and featureless, like living statues.

And in their hands, they carried staffs tipped with crystals that pulsed with a soft, rhythmic glow.

Ethan took a step back, his instincts screaming at him to run.

The figures stopped just a few feet away. One of them—a tall figure with an ornate mask resembling a bird's beak—raised a hand. The gesture wasn't hostile, but commanding.

Ethan's pulse raced. He had no idea what to do. Were they friendly? Dangerous?

Then, the figure spoke.

The words were unintelligible—fluid and lyrical, spoken in a language Ethan had never heard before. But something about the cadence, the rhythm, felt strangely... familiar. As if he had heard it before, in a dream long forgotten.

The figure tilted its head slightly, waiting for a response.

Ethan's mouth was dry. He had no idea how to answer.

"I—I don't understand," he stammered, his voice hoarse.

The figure exchanged a glance with the others, then took a step closer. This time, when it spoke, the words seemed to shift, almost as if they were rearranging themselves in his mind.

"You... are not of this time."

Ethan's breath hitched.

"*You understand me?*"

The figure nodded.

"*You carry the Watch.*"

Ethan glanced down at the pocket watch still clutched in his fingers.

"*What is this thing? What did it do to me?*"

The figure paused. Then, with a slow, deliberate motion, it lifted a hand and gestured toward the massive stone archway behind Ethan—the one he hadn't noticed until now.

It was carved from the same dark stone as the surrounding buildings, but its surface pulsed with veins of golden light. Strange symbols glowed along its edges, shifting, changing, alive. It was shaped like a gateway, a door standing in the middle of nothingness.

"*The Time Gate,*" the figure said.

Ethan's stomach twisted.

"*It brought you here.*"

His mind reeled. He turned to the archway, then back to the robed figures.

"Can it send me back?"

The figure hesitated.

"Not without the Watch's power."

Ethan's grip tightened around the pocket watch.

"Then how do I fix it?"

For the first time, the figure's voice held a trace of something new—something Ethan couldn't quite place.

"You must learn the truth."

The wind picked up, rustling the robes of the gathered figures. The golden light of the Time Gate shimmered, its energy pulsing in slow, deliberate waves.

Ethan swallowed hard.

The truth.

Whatever that meant, he had no choice but to find out.

Ethan's mind spun as the figure's words echoed in

his ears. *"You must learn the truth."* The phrase hung in the air like a heavy fog, its meaning just out of reach, teasing him with the promise of something far greater than he had ever anticipated. His heart pounded in his chest, and every instinct screamed for him to retreat, to run back through the archway, to return to the life he knew, where things made sense, where time was predictable. But something—something in the figure's tone, in the pulsing golden light of the Time Gate—compelled him to stay.

Ethan clenched the pocket watch tighter, feeling its warmth seeping into his skin. The ancient device had brought him here, to a world that should not exist, and now, it seemed to be his only connection to whatever reality he had left. What was this place? What was this Time Gate? And what truth was he supposed to uncover?

The figure with the bird-like mask motioned for Ethan to follow, and though every part of him wanted to resist, he found himself stepping forward, his feet moving before he could think to stop them. The robed figures parted to make way, their silent gazes following him as he walked. With each step, the air grew thicker, charged with an energy that vibrated through his body, almost as if the city itself was alive. The stone beneath his feet hummed faintly, reverberating through his bones.

They walked in silence for what felt like hours, the towering buildings of the city looming over them, casting long shadows as the suns began to dip lower in the sky. The landscape around him seemed to pulse with a strange, otherworldly rhythm. It was as though the very fabric of this place was woven from time itself, its threads stretching and folding in ways Ethan could not begin to comprehend. His mind raced, trying to make sense of everything. He had been transported through time—this much was clear. But how? Why him? And what had caused the Time Gate to open in the first place?

Finally, they reached the base of a massive structure that loomed before them, its walls stretching impossibly high, lost in the mist above. The building was made of the same dark stone, but unlike the others, this one seemed to glow faintly from within, casting an ethereal light across the ground. The symbols carved into its surface were much more intricate, almost as if they were alive, shifting and moving in ways that defied logic.

The tall figure with the bird mask raised a hand toward the entrance. At his gesture, the large stone doors slowly creaked open, revealing a vast, circular chamber inside. The room was illuminated by the soft, pulsating glow of crystals embedded into the walls, their light casting strange shadows that danced along the floor. In the center of the room stood a raised platform, upon which rested a large, intricately carved stone table.

Ethan's breath caught as he stepped into the chamber. There, standing in front of the table, was a figure unlike any he had seen before. This one wore no mask, and its face was serene, almost otherworldly. Its eyes were deep pools of silver, shimmering with knowledge that seemed to reach far beyond the limits of time and space. The figure was tall, dressed in flowing robes of dark blue, and its presence radiated a quiet power.

The figure turned to face Ethan, and though no words were spoken, a sense of recognition flooded him. This being—the one standing before him—seemed familiar, as though Ethan had known it for lifetimes. Its gaze held him, steady and unwavering, and for a moment, time itself seemed to stretch out before him, as if the world around him had fallen away.

Finally, the figure spoke, its voice soft but clear. *"You have come, Ethan."*

Ethan's throat went dry, his mouth unable to form words. He stood frozen, staring at the being, uncertain of what to say. The only thing he could think was: *How does it know my name?*

"You were chosen," the figure continued, its voice like the hum of ancient winds. *"Chosen by the Watch, chosen by time itself. Your arrival was foreseen long ago, written in the very fabric of existence."*

Ethan's mind reeled. *Chosen?* He felt his knees weaken, the weight of the situation crashing down on him. The Watch had *chosen* him? How was that possible? What did it mean?

"What do you mean? How—?" Ethan's voice faltered, and he struggled to find the right words.

The figure raised a hand, silencing him. *"You will understand in time. But first, you must see."*

Ethan watched, transfixed, as the figure reached out toward the stone table in the center of the room. As if responding to its touch, the surface of the table shimmered, and a swirling image appeared above it—an intricate map, glowing with soft light. The map was unlike any map Ethan had ever seen, its lines and symbols constantly shifting and rearranging themselves, moving as if they were alive.

"*This is the map of time,*" the figure explained, its voice reverberating in the chamber. "*A map that shows the flow of all things—the rise and fall of civilizations, the ebb and flow of history, the lives of those who came before, and the paths of those who will come after. But it is more than just a map.*"

The figure paused, and its gaze fell upon the Watch in Ethan's hand. The golden light in the room seemed to intensify, and for the first time, Ethan noticed that the Watch was pulsing, responding to the map as if it were connected to it.

"The Watch," the figure said softly, "*is a key. A key that can unlock the paths within this map. It holds the power to travel through time, but it is not just a tool. It is a part of you now. Its power is your power, and with it, you will shape the future.*"

Ethan's mind raced. *Shaped the future?* His heart thudded against his chest. He had been tossed into this world, this strange and ancient place, and now he was being told that he had the power to change history? To alter time itself?

"But there is a danger," the figure continued, its silver eyes darkening. *"The Watch is not the only key to this power. There are others who seek it—others who would use it for destruction. And they will stop at nothing to get it."*

A chill ran down Ethan's spine. He turned the Watch over in his hand, its weight suddenly feeling much heavier than before.

"You must learn," the figure said, *"how to use the Watch, how to navigate the paths of time. You must stop those who would abuse its power. But most of all, you must understand that time is not a force to be taken lightly. The consequences of your actions may ripple through all of existence."*

Ethan's head swam with the enormity of the task before him. *"How do I stop them?"* he asked, his voice barely above a whisper.

The figure's gaze softened. *"You must find the other pieces. The other keys. Only then will you have the strength to protect time and restore balance."*

With that, the figure turned away, the map fading from the table as the chamber grew still. Ethan stood there, stunned, as the weight of the task settled over him like a heavy cloak. The answers were just beyond his reach, and yet they felt so close. The Watch in his hand pulsed once more, and he knew that the journey ahead would take him far beyond anything he could have ever imagined.

He was no longer just a boy who stumbled upon a strange pocket watch. He was now a keeper of time, with the fate of the universe resting in his hands.

And the journey had only just begun.

MEETING THE PRINCESS

Ethan stood frozen, the words of the figure echoing in his mind like a haunting whisper. *"Find the other pieces. Only then will you have the strength to protect time and restore balance."* His fingers tightened around the pocket watch, the familiar weight in his palm a stark reminder that his life had irrevocably changed. But the path ahead was still shrouded in mystery. He had been thrust into a world far beyond his understanding, where time itself seemed to bend and twist in ways that defied logic. The ancient city, the figures in masks, the glowing map—it was all overwhelming. But above all, the figure's warning had settled deeply within him: *Others would stop at nothing to obtain the Watch.*

The air in the chamber grew heavier as Ethan processed the enormity of the task before him. He needed to find the pieces—the other keys—but where would he begin? The Watch had brought him here, but it offered no answers, no clear direction. And what of these mysterious enemies, those who sought to destroy and reshape time for their own gain? Every question seemed to raise another, and Ethan felt more lost with each passing second.

Suddenly, a soft sound, like the rustle of silk, broke the silence. Ethan's head snapped to the side, his heart skipping a beat. A figure had entered the chamber, moving with grace, as if she were part of the very air itself. She was unlike anyone Ethan had seen so far in this strange place—tall and elegant, with long, dark hair that cascaded like a waterfall down her back, her robes shimmering with a delicate blend of blues and silvers. Her presence seemed to fill the room, both calming and powerful at the same time.

But it wasn't just her appearance that struck Ethan; it was her eyes. Deep pools of violet, they seemed to carry the weight of centuries, a look that saw not just him, but through him—straight into the heart of his soul. There was a depth to her gaze, a knowing that made Ethan feel as though she understood everything that had happened to him, and everything that would come.

The figure—no, this woman—approached him with a quiet intensity, her steps measured and deliberate.

She stopped before him, her gaze never wavering, and for a moment, the world seemed to pause. Ethan could feel the weight of her stare, and yet, there was a warmth in it that made him feel, strangely, like he had found someone he could trust.

Finally, she spoke, her voice soft, like a whisper carried on the wind, yet imbued with an unmistakable strength. *"You've come far, Ethan."*

Ethan blinked in surprise. She knew his name—just like the figure in the chamber had. But there was no time to question how. *"Who are you?"* he asked, his voice steady, though his heart raced.

The woman smiled faintly, her lips curving upward in a way that hinted at both wisdom and sorrow. *"I am Lila, princess of this land. The city you stand in, and the world beyond, are not as they seem. And neither is the power you now hold."*

Ethan's breath caught. *Princess?* The weight of her title struck him like a thunderbolt. This was no ordinary woman—she was royalty, yet her presence was so unassuming that it almost seemed out of place. Lila's gaze softened, sensing his confusion. *"I know what you must be thinking. This world is full of mysteries, and your arrival was not by chance. You are here for a reason. But you must understand, the path ahead will not be easy. The dangers are greater than you can imagine."*

Ethan swallowed hard, his mind swirling. "What kind of dangers? What do you mean?"

Lila's expression grew serious, her violet eyes darkening with concern. She stepped closer, her voice dropping to a hushed tone, as though they were not alone in the room. "There are forces in this world—ancient forces—that have been awoken by your arrival. The Time Watch is not just a key to time. It is also a beacon. A beacon that calls to those who would see time itself destroyed. The Watch is the last of its kind, and whoever controls it holds the power to rewrite history, to bend time to their will."

Ethan felt his stomach twist into knots. He had only just begun to understand the significance of the Watch, and now, Lila's words were painting a much darker picture. If there were others who sought the Watch, it wasn't just a matter of collecting the pieces. It was about survival. And not just his own.

Lila took a deep breath, as if steeling herself for what she was about to say. *"There are many who would stop at nothing to obtain the Watch and its power. They are relentless, and their reach extends across all of time. They have already begun to search for the pieces, and they will not hesitate to destroy anyone who stands in their way. That's why you must be careful. You must trust no one except those who are truly aligned with the truth. And even then, you must question everything. Nothing is as it seems here."*

Ethan felt a cold shiver crawl up his spine. Lila's words were filled with an urgency that seemed to grow stronger with every passing second. The weight of her warning was suffocating. *"I don't know what to do,"* Ethan confessed, his voice cracking slightly. *"I don't know where to start. I don't even know who to trust."*

Lila's gaze softened again, and she placed a hand on his shoulder—gentle, yet firm. *"You are not alone in this, Ethan. There are those who will help you, those who believe in the power of the Watch, and in the balance it can restore. But the choices you make will determine the fate of not just this world, but all worlds."*

Her eyes locked with his, and for a moment, Ethan saw the weight of her words settle in her gaze. *"You must be ready. The first piece is close, but so are those who will try to stop you. The journey ahead will test your strength, your courage, and your heart. But you must keep moving forward. The fate of time depends on it."*

Ethan nodded, though doubt still gnawed at him. He felt the crushing weight of responsibility press down on him, but there was something in Lila's words, in the quiet strength of her presence, that stirred a small flame of determination within him.

Lila stepped back, her expression unreadable, as though she had shared all she could for now. *"There is much more to learn, but time is not on our side. You must hurry."* She turned toward the door, but before stepping through, she paused and glanced back at Ethan. *"Trust in yourself. You are the key to the future."*

And with that, she disappeared into the shadows of the chamber, leaving Ethan standing in the midst of the ancient city, alone once more. But this time, there was a new resolve within him. He had a purpose. He had a mission. And no matter the dangers ahead, he would face them head-on. The journey was just beginning, but he wasn't the same person he had been when he first stepped through the Time Gate. He was now part of something much bigger than himself—a force that could change the very fabric of time.

As the echo of Lila's words lingered in his mind, Ethan set his jaw and prepared to face whatever challenges lay ahead. The adventure had only just begun.

Ethan stood in the chamber, his mind racing, long after Lila's departure. The weight of her words hung heavily in the air, their resonance echoing through every corner of his thoughts. *The Watch is a beacon. A key that must be protected at all costs.* He had understood the danger, but now the reality of it settled within him like a cold shiver. If Lila was right—and he had no reason to believe she wasn't—then the enemies he'd barely begun to understand would stop at nothing to get their hands on the Watch. He wasn't just carrying an ancient artifact; he was carrying the future of time itself.

A part of him felt small, insignificant, but that same part was quickly being replaced with a quiet, burning resolve. Lila had spoken of the pieces, of the dangers, and of those who would seek to control the Watch. Yet, she had also mentioned allies. People who would stand with him. As overwhelming as it all seemed, Ethan knew one thing for sure: he was no longer just an observer in this world. He was a player in something far larger than himself—a battle for the very fabric of existence.

With Lila's warning fresh in his mind, he made a decision. He would not stand idle. He would find these pieces, whatever they were, and he would protect the Watch at all costs. But where to begin?

The city was ancient—its stone buildings weathered by centuries, yet they stood with an unyielding pride, as though they had seen the rise and fall of empires, watched the turning of countless eras. The streets wound in intricate patterns, twisting like a labyrinth. He could hear the hum of a life he hadn't fully understood yet, a life in this strange world where time itself seemed fractured. But there was no time to waste. He had a mission, and Lila had mentioned that the first piece was close.

Ethan glanced around, his eyes scanning the walls of the chamber. There had to be more clues, more to uncover. He couldn't do this alone. The thought of being plunged deeper into this unknown realm without any guidance felt daunting. But perhaps, if he could find those who had aligned themselves with the Watch—those who understood its power—he might find the answers he so desperately sought.

A sudden movement caught his eye. He turned sharply, his pulse quickening. A figure was emerging from the shadows, cloaked in a dark robe. The figure moved silently, but there was a grace to the way they stepped—like someone who had lived their life in the shadows, waiting for the right moment to reveal themselves.

"Looking for something?" the figure's voice came, low and steady.

Ethan's heart raced, his instincts telling him that this person, whoever they were, knew something about the Watch—maybe even more than Lila had revealed. But how much could he trust them? Was this an ally, or yet another shadow lurking in the dark, waiting for an opportunity to strike?

"I—" Ethan began, but the figure raised a gloved hand, cutting him off.

"Don't speak," the figure said, their voice barely above a whisper. "Not yet. I know why you're here. You're not the first to arrive, but you might be the last if you're not careful." The figure's voice carried an edge of warning, but there was something else in it—something that suggested a kind of knowing, a shared understanding of the perils ahead.

Ethan hesitated. He wanted answers, but he wasn't about to trust just anyone. He had already learned the hard way that appearances could be deceiving. "Who are you?" Ethan asked cautiously, his eyes narrowing as he sized up the mysterious figure.

The cloaked individual did not immediately answer. Instead, they stepped forward, drawing a small object from beneath their cloak—a key, ancient in design but undeniably familiar. The key had intricate markings on it, similar to the ones he had seen on the Watch, as if they belonged to the same language, the same hidden knowledge. The figure held it out to him, and Ethan's breath caught.

"The pieces," the figure said softly. "I have one, and you will need it. It's a part of the puzzle. But it's not just any key—it's a test. The others are hidden, scattered across time and space, but each one can only be unlocked by someone worthy. If you want to protect the Watch and the balance of time, you will need this."

Ethan took the key in his hand, feeling its weight—a weight that was oddly familiar, as if it were calling to him. His fingers brushed the ancient markings, and for a brief moment, his mind seemed to flash with a vision. He saw a landscape, barren and desolate, a land scorched by time. In the distance, a city—shattered, crumbling—lay in ruins, its towers reaching for the sky like broken fingers. But the vision was fleeting, gone as quickly as it had appeared.

"What does this mean?" Ethan asked, his voice filled with a mixture of awe and confusion.

The figure's eyes gleamed from beneath their hood. "It means you're not the only one searching for the pieces. There are others who want to see time destroyed, who believe the Watch can give them control over all of it. They will stop at nothing to possess it. But you have an advantage, Ethan. You have the Watch, and you have the heart to protect it. Don't lose that."

Ethan felt a sudden rush of emotions—fear, determination, uncertainty—but above all, a strange sense of urgency. *Time was running out.*

The figure turned, ready to leave, but not before they said one final thing.

"The first piece is closer than you think. Trust in what you see. But remember, appearances can deceive." And with that, the figure disappeared back into the shadows.

Ethan stood there, still holding the key. His mind was a whirlwind, the pieces of the puzzle slowly starting to fit together. The mysterious figure had given him a piece, but that only raised more questions. How was this piece connected to the Watch? And why did the figure speak of "appearances deceiving"? What did it mean?

He didn't have all the answers, but one thing was certain—he was no longer alone in this. Whatever lay ahead, he was going to need to trust in himself, in the people he met, and in the strange, cryptic clues that were being laid before him.

As Ethan stood in the center of the ancient city, a plan began to form in his mind. It was time to find the first piece. Time to set this adventure into motion. But as he took his first step into the unknown, he couldn't shake the feeling that the real journey had only just begun.

Ethan stood still, his thoughts swirling with the cryptic words of the mysterious cloaked figure. The key he held felt almost alive in his palm, pulsing with an energy that made his skin tingle. His mind raced—he was in a strange city, far from everything he had ever known, with no idea what was coming next. Lila had warned him, but this—this was something different. The pieces, the key, the enemies lurking in the shadows—it was all starting to form a picture in his mind, but it was a picture of something he wasn't sure he was ready to face.

He glanced down at the key, its markings glowing faintly in the dim light of the chamber. There was no doubt that it was linked to the Watch. But what was its purpose? And how was he supposed to find the other pieces? And more importantly, what would happen if he failed?

His thoughts were interrupted by a soft sound—a rustling of footsteps approaching from behind. He turned quickly, his instincts on high alert, but it wasn't the cloaked figure again. It was someone else—someone he had never expected to meet in a place like this.

Standing in the doorway of the chamber was Lila. Her presence was commanding, even more so than when they first met. She had shed her earlier urgency, her posture now calm and collected, as though she had prepared herself for the next stage of their journey. Her eyes locked onto his with a seriousness that sent a chill down his spine.

"Ethan," Lila said, her voice steady but with an edge of concern, "We don't have much time."

Ethan's heart skipped a beat. "What's going on?" he asked, his voice sounding weaker than he intended.

Lila walked into the room, her eyes scanning the key in his hand before meeting his gaze once more. "That key you're holding is part of something much bigger than you realize," she said, her voice quieter now. "It's one of the pieces that will either protect time or destroy it. But there are those who would use it for far darker purposes."

Ethan took a deep breath, feeling the weight of her words pressing down on him. "I know I'm supposed to find the other pieces," he said, his voice tinged with uncertainty. "But what happens if I don't?"

Lila's expression softened, but only for a moment. "If you don't," she began, her voice steady, "then time as we know it will unravel. The Watch is a beacon—a key to controlling not only time but the very fabric of reality. If it falls into the wrong hands, it will destroy everything."

The silence that followed was heavy. Ethan could hear the distant echo of his own heartbeat, the tension in the air thick and suffocating. Lila continued, her tone somber but resolute.

"There are forces here—ancient, powerful forces—that have been waiting for someone like you. Someone who holds the Watch. You are the only one who can keep it from falling into the wrong hands, but you cannot do it alone."

Ethan's mind was spinning. "I can't do this alone? But... you've been helping me all along. What's next?"

Lila's eyes softened, her voice dropping to a whisper as she stepped closer to Ethan. "There are others—people who have the knowledge, the power, and the experience to help you. They're scattered across time and space, but the first one—the first ally—you need to find is here, in this city."

Ethan's brow furrowed. "Who?"

Lila hesitated, as if weighing the gravity of her next words. "Princess Mirena," she said finally, her eyes serious. "She is the guardian of the city and the key to unlocking the next phase of your journey. But she is not just any princess. She is tied to the Watch, just as you are. Her fate and yours are intertwined. You must find her—before the others do."

A chill ran down Ethan's spine. A princess? This was all becoming too much. How was he supposed to find her in a city like this, surrounded by strange architecture and people who spoke in riddles? He barely knew where to start, let alone how to find someone so important.

"Where is she?" he asked, his voice barely above a whisper.

Lila's gaze turned towards the far corner of the room, where a large tapestry hung against the wall, depicting a battle scene with warriors on horseback, the sky dark with storm clouds. "She is close," Lila said softly. "But the city is vast, and many would go to great lengths to keep her hidden. You will need to use the key to find her. It will guide you—if you can read its messages."

Ethan looked down at the key in his hand, its surface still pulsing with an almost imperceptible glow. He had no idea how this small object could possibly guide him to someone as important as a princess, but he had no choice but to trust Lila's words. He had to move forward, no matter how daunting it seemed.

"Take this," Lila said, extending a small map to him. It was old, frayed at the edges, and covered in strange symbols that Ethan couldn't read. "It's a map of the city, but it's more than just directions. It's a guide to the hidden paths, the places that are off-limits to most people. You'll need to find her quickly, before others do."

Ethan took the map from her, nodding solemnly. The weight of the task ahead of him was starting to feel almost unbearable, but he had no other choice. This was the world he had stumbled into, and if he wanted to survive, he had to play by its rules.

"Thank you," he said quietly, his eyes meeting hers. "I'll find her. I won't let the Watch fall into the wrong hands."

Lila's lips curved into a faint smile. "I know you won't." Her eyes lingered on him for a moment, as if assessing his resolve. "But remember, Ethan, not everyone in this city is your ally. The Watch is a powerful force, and there are those who would kill to get their hands on it. Be careful."

With those words, she turned and walked towards the door, her figure fading into the shadows. As the door clicked shut behind her, Ethan stood alone in the chamber, the key and the map in his hands. The room felt colder now, and the weight of the mission ahead was pressing heavily on his chest.

He knew one thing for sure: finding Princess Mirena would not be easy. The city was vast, and he had no idea where to begin. But Lila's words echoed in his mind, and he knew this was the only path forward. If he was going to protect the Watch, if he was going to prevent time from unraveling, he had to find her—before it was too late.

With a final glance at the map, Ethan stepped out into the city, ready to face whatever challenges awaited him.

THE LOST CITY'S SECRET

Ethan stood in the midst of the ancient city, the weight of his mission settling over him like a heavy cloak. The map in his hand felt like it was growing heavier with each passing moment. He couldn't shake the feeling that the city, with its vastness and eerie silence, was somehow watching him—waiting for him to make the next move. The streets stretched out before him, bathed in the warm, golden light of the late afternoon. The architecture of the city was unlike anything he had seen before—towering stone structures covered in intricate carvings, depicting scenes of long-forgotten battles, celestial symbols, and strange figures that seemed to move in the shadows of the walls.

He turned his attention back to the map, trying to make sense of the strange symbols that danced across its surface. The city was divided into sections, each more mysterious than the last. The map seemed to hint at places that were off-limits—hidden chambers, underground tunnels, and sacred sites that were shrouded in secrecy. As Ethan studied the map, his thoughts wandered back to what Lila had told him.

The Watch. The key. The princess.

The more he thought about it, the more he realized just how little he understood. Why was he the one chosen for this mission? Why had the Watch appeared to him of all people? And what connection did the city have to time travel? Ethan's mind raced with questions, but there were no easy answers. The only way forward was to explore the city, follow the map, and uncover the truth.

His first step was to find the Library of Ages, a place mentioned on the map that was said to hold the city's most ancient secrets. The library was located in the heart of the city, behind massive gates made of silver and adorned with symbols that pulsed with an energy that felt almost alive. As he approached the gates, a sense of foreboding washed over him. He had no idea what awaited him inside, but he knew it was the next step in his journey.

The gates opened with a soft, metallic creak as Ethan stepped forward, his footsteps echoing in the silence. The library was vast, its shelves stretching endlessly into the shadows. The air was thick with the scent of ancient parchment, and the dim light of the setting sun filtered through tall, narrow windows, casting long shadows on the stone floor. The atmosphere was heavy with the weight of knowledge, the kind of knowledge that had been passed down through the ages, carefully guarded and protected from the outside world.

Ethan wandered deeper into the library, his eyes scanning the rows of books and scrolls that lined the shelves. Some of the books were ancient, their bindings cracked and faded, while others were newer, their pages still crisp and white. As he wandered further, he stumbled upon a large stone pedestal in the center of the room. Resting atop it was a massive tome, its cover adorned with the same celestial symbols he had seen etched into the city's walls.

The book seemed to call to him.

Ethan approached cautiously, his fingers brushing lightly against the cover. The moment his touch made contact, the book's pages began to turn on their own, as if guided by some unseen force. The air around him seemed to hum with energy, and the symbols on the pages glowed faintly, illuminating the dark corners of the library.

He began to read, his eyes quickly absorbing the words as though they were written just for him. The text described the history of the city—an ancient civilization that had once thrived at the crossroads of time and space. According to the book, the city was built upon the ruins of a forgotten empire, one that had discovered the secret to manipulating time itself. The citizens of the city had learned to travel through time, to bend the very fabric of reality to their will.

But with this power came great responsibility—and great danger.

The city's leaders had known that the power of time travel was too great to be wielded by any one person. So, they constructed the Watch—a device capable of controlling time and preventing anyone from abusing its power. The Watch was divided into several pieces, each hidden away in secret locations across time and space. Only those with the key, like Ethan, could unlock the Watch's power and use it to protect time from those who would seek to destroy it.

As Ethan continued to read, he learned that the city had been the epicenter of countless time-altering events. The citizens of the city had traveled to distant eras, witnessing the rise and fall of empires, the birth of new worlds, and the destruction of old ones. They had been the keepers of time, ensuring that history unfolded as it should. But eventually, the city had fallen into ruin. The knowledge of time travel had been lost, the people scattered across time, leaving behind only fragments of their once-great civilization.

The final pages of the book revealed a startling truth: The city's connection to time travel was not just a matter of history—it was a living, breathing force that still existed within the city itself. The buildings, the streets, the very air seemed to pulse with the energy of time. The key to controlling this power, the Watch, was not just an artifact—it was the heart of the city, and its power could only be unlocked by those destined to wield it.

Ethan's mind spun as the implications of what he had just read began to sink in. The city itself was a part of the Watch. The city was alive, and its connection to time was far deeper than he had ever imagined. But there was more—much more. If the Watch were to fall into the wrong hands, if the city's secret were uncovered by those who sought to use its power for evil, the fabric of time itself could unravel, destroying everything.

The book closed with a final, chilling warning: *The time of reckoning is near. The Watch will either save or destroy us all.*

Ethan's heart pounded in his chest. He had to find the Watch, and he had to do it quickly. The stakes were higher than he had ever realized. The city's secret was not just about protecting time—it was about protecting reality itself.

As he turned away from the pedestal, the shadows in the library seemed to grow longer, darker. The air grew colder, and Ethan could feel the weight of the city's secret pressing down on him. He wasn't sure how much longer he could stay in this place, how much longer he could search for answers before the city's hidden dangers found him first.

But he knew one thing for sure: The city's secret had been revealed, and there was no turning back now.

As Ethan stepped away from the ancient book, the weight of the information pressing against his chest felt almost physical. He could still hear the soft rustling of the book's pages turning by themselves, as if it had a life of its own—a sentiment that seemed less far-fetched the deeper he delved into the city's mysteries. Each step Ethan took seemed to echo louder in the library, as if the very structure of the city was listening, waiting for him to make his next move.

He couldn't shake the feeling that the city itself was a living, breathing entity, its pulse inextricably tied to the workings of time itself. As he stood there, pondering the enormity of what he had learned, a deep, uneasy silence seemed to fill the air. The hum of energy that had once enveloped the library now felt subdued, almost as though it was waiting for something—or someone—to set the next event into motion.

Ethan knew he couldn't stay in the library forever. His mind was racing with the possibilities of what lay ahead. If the Watch was indeed the key to controlling time, then its secrets could not remain locked away for long. Someone or something would come looking for it, and that was something he couldn't risk. Time itself, as he now understood it, was fragile. The very fabric of existence was in the balance, and if he failed, everything could crumble.

But first, he had to find the Watch.

The book had mentioned its location in cryptic terms—the heart of the city, hidden beneath the streets. Ethan's eyes searched the library again, but the place seemed no more helpful now than it had been when he first entered. The city's corridors stretched endlessly, and each corner he turned felt more disorienting than the last. It was as though he was standing at the center of a maze—one designed not just to disorient but to test him.

Suddenly, a voice echoed from the shadows of the library, breaking the tension in the air.

"You've found it, haven't you?" The voice was soft, almost a whisper, but it carried a weight of certainty.

Ethan spun around, his heart racing, and there she was—Lila. She stepped out from behind one of the tall bookshelves, her features half-obscured in the dim light. She moved with an air of grace, but there was something in her eyes that made Ethan pause. It was as if she knew something he didn't.

Lila looked at him, her expression unreadable, but there was an underlying sense of urgency in her voice as she spoke again.

"The Watch… you're not the only one searching for it. You need to be careful. There are those who would use it for their own purposes—those who believe they can rewrite history." Her eyes scanned the ancient walls of the library, and for a moment, Ethan swore he saw a flicker of fear in them. "And if they succeed… everything we know could be lost."

Ethan could feel the weight of her words. He had known from the moment he stepped through the time gate that this journey wasn't going to be easy. But Lila's warning made the situation even more dire than he had imagined. He wasn't just up against the clock—he was up against an enemy who would stop at nothing to gain control of the power that lay hidden in the city.

Lila stepped closer to him, her movements deliberate. "There's a place," she said, lowering her voice even further, "a hidden chamber beneath the city where the Watch is kept. It's protected by an ancient force, one that even time itself cannot erase. But it won't be easy to reach. The city will try to stop you. It's designed to defend itself, to keep those who are not worthy from unlocking its secrets."

Ethan glanced at her, his thoughts swirling. The puzzle pieces were slowly falling into place. The city wasn't just an ancient metropolis—it was a fortress. A living, breathing entity that existed to guard the most powerful secrets of all. The Watch was the key to understanding not just the city's history, but time itself.

Lila seemed to sense his thoughts, her voice turning solemn. "There are others here, Ethan. People who are also seeking the Watch. They won't hesitate to use you, to manipulate you, if it means gaining access to its power."

Ethan looked at her, trying to gauge her sincerity. What had drawn Lila to this place? Was she a mere guide, or did she have an ulterior motive? Her warnings were real, but he couldn't shake the feeling that she knew more than she was letting on.

As if reading his mind, Lila gave him a slight smile—a rare gesture that made her appear less like an enigma and more like a human. "You don't have to trust me completely," she said. "But I'm offering you a chance. A chance to find the Watch before anyone else does. You'll need me if you want to survive."

The gravity of the situation settled in. Ethan knew she was right. He couldn't do this alone, not in a city where time itself seemed to be in a constant state of flux. But as he looked at her, he couldn't help but wonder—was Lila truly an ally, or was there more to her story than she was revealing?

For a moment, the silence stretched between them, the weight of the decision pressing on Ethan's shoulders. He had to decide. Trust Lila and risk walking into the unknown, or go it alone and risk falling into the hands of those who would destroy everything?

The air around him seemed to thicken, the hum of time shifting once more. It was as if the city itself was waiting for his choice, for his next move.

"I'll need your help," Ethan said finally, his voice steady despite the uncertainty gnawing at his gut. "But we need to be careful. I can't let anyone find the Watch before I do."

Lila's eyes glinted with an unreadable emotion, but she nodded. "Then we have no time to lose. Follow me, Ethan. I'll show you the way."

As she turned and began walking deeper into the library, Ethan hesitated for a moment before following her. His mind was still swirling with questions, but one thing was clear: He was no longer just a visitor in this city. He was now a part of its history, caught in the balance of time itself. The journey ahead was fraught with danger, but the stakes were higher than he could have ever imagined.

As they ventured deeper into the city's heart, the shadows seemed to grow longer, more oppressive. The air was thick with the sense of ancient power—

power that had been dormant for centuries, waiting for someone like Ethan to awaken it.

And so, their journey continued.

Ethan followed Lila through the winding corridors of the ancient city, each step taking them deeper into its heart. The atmosphere was heavy with the weight of forgotten centuries, and the silence around them was palpable. It felt as though the very walls of the city were holding their breath, as if the place itself was aware of their presence, watching them with an unseen eye. There were no windows, no light except for the faint glow that emanated from the moss-covered stones underfoot. Every so often, the faint hum of the city would rise again, vibrating through the stone like a heartbeat, but then it would fall silent, as if afraid to disturb the tranquility of the ancient place.

Lila led Ethan to a narrow passageway, hidden beneath an archway adorned with intricate carvings of timepieces, celestial bodies, and symbols he didn't recognize. These markings were unlike anything he had ever seen, and as he studied them, his mind raced with questions. They seemed to tell a story—one of creation, decay, and renewal, stretching across the fabric of time. They depicted moments of great importance, perhaps key events that had shaped the city's history, or the very essence of time travel itself. But there was no time to dwell on their meaning now; Lila's urgency was clear.

"This way," she said quietly, her voice carrying a tone of warning. Her eyes darted around the shadows as if expecting something to emerge from the darkness at any moment. She didn't need to say more. Ethan could feel the tension rising between them, the atmosphere thick with danger.

They descended further into the depths of the city, where the air grew cooler and more oppressive. The architecture around them shifted. The stone was no longer smooth and polished but rough and jagged, as if the deeper they went, the older and more primal the city became. The flickering of Lila's lantern was their only guide as they ventured through the winding maze of passages.

After what felt like hours, they reached a large chamber, its ceiling vaulted high above them, lost in the shadows. The floor was covered in dust, and the air was thick with the scent of age and decay. At the far end of the chamber was an immense door, unlike anything Ethan had seen in the city so far. It was made of a dark metal, intricately wrought with patterns that seemed to shift and change when he looked at them. Symbols of time—gears, clocks, and swirling cosmic designs—intertwined with one another, giving the door an almost living appearance.

"This is it," Lila said, her voice reverberating slightly in the cavernous space. "The entrance to the inner sanctum."

Ethan's breath caught in his throat. He could feel the weight of history pressing down on him, the weight of everything that had brought him here. The Watch was behind that door, waiting for him—waiting for someone worthy enough to wield its power. He felt an overwhelming sense of responsibility, as if he were standing on the precipice of something that could alter the course of history itself.

Lila moved forward and placed her hand on the door, her fingers tracing the shifting symbols. The door responded, the symbols glowing faintly, almost as if recognizing her touch. She turned to Ethan, her face illuminated by the soft, ethereal light.

"You don't understand the magnitude of what's behind this door," she said, her voice suddenly quieter, more intense. "The Watch is not just a device. It's a key to the very fabric of time. Whoever controls it controls history itself. But it's not just about power. It's about balance. Time is fragile, Ethan. If we tamper with it too much, the consequences could be devastating."

Ethan nodded, his heart racing. He could feel the weight of her words, the importance of what lay before him. It wasn't just about finding the Watch—it was about understanding its true purpose. But what was its true purpose? Was it really something to be controlled, or was it a force that should be left untouched?

As Lila stepped back, she motioned for Ethan to approach. He moved toward the door, his heart pounding in his chest. The closer he got, the stronger the pull seemed to be. It was as if the city itself was drawing him toward it, urging him to unlock its secrets. His fingers brushed against the cold metal of the door, and he felt a sudden surge of energy pulse through him. It was as though the Watch was calling to him, its presence vibrating in the air, demanding his attention.

Lila looked at him, her expression hardening. "Once you open this door, there's no turning back. The city will react. It will test you, Ethan. And you'll be forced to make a choice. Are you truly ready for what lies beyond?"

He hesitated, the enormity of her words sinking in. This was it. This was the moment that would change everything. He had come this far, and there was no turning back now. The Watch was within his reach, and he had to understand its power before it fell into the wrong hands.

With a deep breath, Ethan placed his hand on the door, feeling the cold, ancient metal beneath his fingers. The symbols shifted once more, their glow intensifying. The air around him seemed to shimmer, and the faint hum of time returned, louder than ever before. The door began to creak, slowly at first, and then with a mighty groan, it began to open, revealing a darkened passageway beyond.

As the door fully opened, a rush of wind swept through the chamber, carrying with it a strange, intoxicating scent—like the scent of old books and forgotten memories. The path ahead was shrouded in darkness, but Ethan felt an undeniable pull toward it. His heart raced, his mind filled with questions, but above all, a sense of anticipation gripped him.

This was it. The moment of truth. Beyond the door lay the heart of the lost city, and with it, the answers he had been seeking. But what would he find when he stepped into that darkness? And what price would he have to pay for the power of the Watch?

Lila stood by his side, her expression unreadable. "Remember, Ethan," she said softly, her voice tinged with something he couldn't quite place. "The city will show you what you're truly made of. Be careful what you seek, for some truths are better left uncovered."

With those final words hanging in the air, Ethan took a step forward, crossing the threshold into the unknown. The door behind him slammed shut, sealing him inside.

The journey had only just begun.

THE TYRANT KING

Ethan stepped cautiously through the darkened corridor, his footsteps echoing softly against the cold stone walls of the ancient city. The air grew heavy, thick with a sense of foreboding as he ventured deeper into the heart of the lost city. Each step seemed to bring him closer to something monumental—something that had been hidden away for centuries, its power too dangerous for the world to bear.

Lila walked beside him, her face pale in the dim light, her eyes clouded with concern. The weight of what lay ahead was evident in her every movement. She seemed to be fighting something—perhaps the urge to warn Ethan further, or maybe the reluctance to delve deeper into the past that haunted this city. But she said nothing more. Instead, she led him forward, her lantern casting eerie shadows along the walls as they passed.

The corridor widened into a vast hall, its ceiling soaring high above them, supported by massive pillars that looked as if they had been carved from a single, colossal stone. The walls were adorned with faded murals, their images now little more than ghostly remnants of a time long gone. But even in their fragmented state, they told a chilling tale.

Ethan could make out figures in the paintings—elaborate ceremonies, kings seated upon thrones, and people bowing in reverence. One figure in particular stood out: a tall, imposing man draped in dark robes, his eyes gleaming with ambition and cold resolve. The more Ethan studied the mural, the more he felt a chill run down his spine. There was something undeniably sinister about the man's gaze—something that made his heart race with a growing sense of dread. This was no ordinary king.

"This is the throne room," Lila whispered, her voice barely audible in the silence. "Where the rulers of this city once held court. But it's more than that. This is where the city's true power was forged."

Ethan's curiosity deepened, but before he could ask more, Lila stopped abruptly. She turned to him, her face etched with concern. "You need to understand something, Ethan. The king you saw in those murals… he's not just a ruler. He's a tyrant. And his obsession with controlling time is what led to the downfall of this city."

Ethan frowned. The pieces of the puzzle were starting to fall into place, but there was still so much he didn't understand. "What do you mean? How does he control time?"

Lila's eyes flickered toward the darkened throne at the far end of the room. It was an ornate chair, carved from what looked like obsidian, with sharp edges and intricate engravings that seemed to pulse with a strange energy. "King Darius," she began, her voice low and heavy with the weight of the story, "discovered the power of the Time Gate long before you did. He saw it as a way to secure his rule, to bend time to his will. But what he didn't realize was that time is not something that can be controlled. It's a force that demands respect."

Ethan's heart raced. The realization hit him like a jolt of electricity. The Time Gate wasn't just a gateway to other places—it was a gateway to *everything*. To the past, the future, and the very fabric of existence itself. But with that kind of power, who could resist the temptation to shape history in their own image?

Lila continued, her voice now tinged with sorrow. "King Darius began using the Time Gate to manipulate the events of the past, altering the city's history, changing the course of battles, and bending people to his will. He was obsessed with control, with creating a perfect world where he ruled eternally."

Ethan shook his head in disbelief. "But that's impossible, isn't it? You can't just change time like that."

Lila's gaze hardened. "You're right. That's why the city fell into ruin. Darius's interference with time fractured the very structure of the world. Time itself became unstable, and reality began to break down. It's why the city was abandoned, why it was hidden away from the world. The people fled, and the city's power was sealed to prevent anyone from making the same mistakes."

Ethan stood there, stunned by the gravity of her words. He had thought he was seeking answers to the mysteries of the Time Gate, but now he understood the truth. It wasn't just about exploring the past or the future—it was about preventing a catastrophe. King Darius's thirst for control over time had nearly destroyed everything. And now, that same power was within his reach.

"Darius... He's still alive?" Ethan asked, his voice trembling slightly. The thought of the tyrant king still holding sway over this lost city, still seeking control over time, was almost too much to comprehend.

Lila's eyes narrowed. "No. Darius may not be physically alive, but his influence remains. He left behind a legacy of power, a force that still resonates throughout the city. And now, someone else is searching for it—someone who believes they can harness that power without the same consequences."

Ethan felt a chill spread through him. The danger was far greater than he had imagined. It wasn't just about unlocking the secrets of the Time Gate—it was about stopping a tyrant's legacy from rising again. And he, it seemed, had been chosen to stop it.

"But who's searching for the power now?" Ethan asked, his mind racing with the possibilities. "Who else would dare to use the Time Gate?"

Lila hesitated, her eyes flickering to the shadows that seemed to stretch and twist around them. "There are others," she said quietly. "Other travelers, other seekers who believe they can control time without suffering the same fate as Darius. But they are wrong. And if they succeed, the consequences will be worse than anything you can imagine."

Ethan's heart pounded in his chest as he realized the magnitude of the challenge before him. The Time Gate was more than just a relic of the past—it was the key to the future. And if the wrong hands got hold of it, the world itself could be undone.

"We have to stop them," Ethan said, his voice resolute.

Lila nodded, her expression grim. "We will. But first, you need to understand the full extent of what you're dealing with. The Watch, the gate, the power of time—it all connects back to Darius. He was the first to unlock its potential, but his actions led to a broken reality. We cannot afford to repeat his mistakes."

As they stood in the heart of the lost city, Ethan could feel the weight of Lila's words pressing down on him. He had come here searching for answers, but what he had uncovered was far more dangerous than he had ever imagined. King Darius's quest for ultimate control over time had not only ruined a city—it had created a legacy of destruction that could unravel the very fabric of existence. And now, it was up to Ethan to prevent history from repeating itself.

But time was a fickle thing, and even now, it was slipping away.

Ethan's thoughts churned with the revelation that King Darius's legacy had cast a long shadow over the lost city—and perhaps, over time itself. The weight of Lila's words hung in the air, thick with the gravity of what was at stake. He had come here seeking answers, thinking the Time Gate held only the potential to explore the past, maybe even alter his own future. But now, it was clear: this was far more than a mere portal between time. This was a powerful, volatile force, one that could distort the very fabric of reality.

Lila stood beside him, her eyes scanning the throne room with an intensity that suggested a deeper, personal connection to the history of this place. Her posture, though steady, betrayed an unspoken unease. It was as if the air around them was charged with the echo of past events—whispers of betrayal, ambition, and failure. And all of it, it seemed, had led back to Darius.

"This place..." Ethan began, struggling to keep his voice steady, "it's not just a city, is it? It's a monument to something far darker than I ever imagined."

Lila's gaze softened, and she nodded solemnly. "This city was a beacon of knowledge once—filled with scholars, artisans, and explorers who discovered the secrets of time. They were the ones who built the Time Gate, not out of a desire for power, but out of a thirst for understanding. They believed time could be a tool for progress, for healing. But Darius twisted that knowledge."

The echo of her words hung in the silence between them, as the history of the city unfolded like a tragic tale. Ethan felt a shiver run through him as he realized the true nature of Darius's actions. What had begun as a noble pursuit—unlocking the mysteries of time—had turned into an obsession.

Time was no longer a force to be understood but a weapon to be wielded.

Lila continued, her voice steady but laden with sorrow. "When Darius first discovered the potential of the Time Gate, it was like nothing the world had ever seen. He saw it as a way to break free of the limitations of mortality—to rule across centuries, to change the course of history as he saw fit. He believed that by controlling time, he could create a perfect kingdom, where no enemies could challenge his reign. Where he would be immortal."

Ethan's mind reeled with the implications. "But immortality... It's impossible, isn't it? Time doesn't work like that. You can't just freeze it in your favor."

Lila's eyes flashed, and for a moment, Ethan saw something fierce in her gaze, something that made him realize just how much she had seen in her life. "Darius didn't see it that way. He thought he could bend time to his will, that he could twist its flow to suit his desires. And for a time, he succeeded."

"Until it all fell apart," Ethan added, the pieces of the story beginning to slot into place.

Lila nodded gravely. "Yes. What Darius didn't understand—what no one could foresee—was that time is not something that can be controlled. It's a current that can't be forced, a force that cannot be contained. The more he manipulated it, the more unstable the fabric of reality became. Events began to fracture. The very nature of time itself began to unravel. And with that unraveling came destruction."

The throne room seemed to grow colder as she spoke. Ethan could almost feel the reverberations of past disasters—of kings and queens, of lives torn apart by an unstoppable force. The murals on the walls, faded as they were, now felt more like warnings than remnants of a glorious past. This wasn't just a tale of a kingdom fallen—it was the cautionary tale of a man who sought to rule not just over land and people, but over the very flow of time itself.

Ethan took a deep breath, trying to steady the storm of thoughts that raged within him. He could feel the weight of Lila's words pressing down on him, the burden of the truth. It wasn't just about the Time Gate anymore. It wasn't just about the incredible, forbidden power he had stumbled upon. It was about stopping a repeating cycle—one that had doomed a once-great civilization and could destroy the world as they knew it if he didn't act.

"But if Darius is gone," Ethan asked slowly, his voice full of unease, "what's left? What's stopping anyone else from trying to use the Gate again? From repeating his mistakes?"

Lila's face grew tight, her eyes scanning the shadows around them. "That's what terrifies me," she said softly. "Even though Darius's reign ended, his legacy did not die with him. His obsession with time didn't just vanish. His influence still lingers, hidden beneath the surface, like a dormant flame waiting to be reignited. And there are others—those who would be foolish enough to try to use the Time Gate for their own gain."

Ethan felt a growing sense of dread. He had walked into this city, thinking that the greatest challenge was simply understanding how to use the Time Gate. But now he realized that the true danger was not just its existence—it was the temptation it held for those who sought power beyond measure.

Lila turned to him, her voice now filled with a quiet intensity. "There is a danger, Ethan. A real one. If someone—someone with enough ambition—were to access the Time Gate, they could rewrite history. They could reshape the past, the present, and the future. And once time is altered, there's no telling what might happen. The world we know could cease to exist, replaced by a reality where Darius's vision reigns supreme."

Ethan felt his blood run cold. "So, the real enemy isn't just Darius's ghost, but anyone who finds this place, anyone who understands its power…"

"Exactly." Lila's voice was steady, but there was a trace of something deeper in her eyes—something dark, as though she had seen firsthand the destructive potential of those who sought to control time. "We have to stop them before they can make the same mistake Darius did."

A long silence stretched between them. Ethan's mind raced with the enormity of the task ahead. The Time Gate wasn't just a doorway to the past—it was a weapon. And weapons, as history had shown, were dangerous when placed in the wrong hands. But

Lila's words had stirred something in him—a sense of responsibility, of purpose. He could not, and would not, let history repeat itself.

"So, what do we do now?" he asked, his voice steady despite the storm of thoughts that threatened to overwhelm him.

Lila looked toward the far end of the throne room, where a set of ancient double doors stood ajar, leading into the depths of the city. "We have to find the other pieces," she said quietly. "The ones that hold the key to controlling the Time Gate. And we must do it before anyone else does."

The weight of their mission hung heavily between them, but as Ethan looked at Lila, he saw something in her eyes that he hadn't seen before—a glimmer of hope. Despite the overwhelming danger, despite the terrifying knowledge of what the Time Gate could unleash, they still had a chance. They still had time.

And that, in itself, was a kind of power.

The flickering torchlight cast long shadows on the ancient stone walls of the throne room as Ethan's heart raced. The reality of what Lila had said settled over him like a dark cloud, suffocating in its weight. King Darius had sought ultimate control over time, and though he was gone, his legacy remained like an ominous specter, still influencing the course of history in ways unimaginable. The Time Gate wasn't just a relic—it was a key to unfathomable power, a tool that could rewrite the very essence of time. And there were others, lurking in the shadows, ready to exploit it for their own gain.

The thought of it terrified Ethan, but what terrified him even more was the realization that he was now a part of this ancient conflict. A part of a war not fought with armies and weapons, but with time itself. The more he thought about it, the more the enormity of his situation weighed down on him. Lila had been right: time wasn't just a force to be understood—it was a weapon to be controlled, and if left unchecked, it could bring about chaos on an unimaginable scale.

"Lila, how do we stop them?" Ethan asked, his voice tight with urgency. "How do we stop those who would seek to control time the way Darius did?"

Lila's gaze hardened, and her hand subconsciously gripped the hilt of the blade at her side. "The first step is understanding what we're up against. Darius was not just a king—he was a master of time, a man who could alter the flow of history with a single decision. But time isn't like a kingdom you can rule with an iron fist. It's a force that moves in ways we don't fully understand, and every time someone tries to control it, it exacts a price."

Ethan frowned. "What price?"

"The more you manipulate time," Lila continued, her voice laced with quiet gravitas, "the more it fights back. The fabric of reality itself starts to tear. The past becomes fractured, the present becomes unstable, and the future begins to fade. Darius thought he could control time without consequence, but the consequences were catastrophic. His kingdom fell apart. People vanished from history, entire timelines were wiped out, and the very fabric of the world began to unravel."

Ethan could feel a chill creeping up his spine as Lila's words sank in. The thought of altering time—of changing even the smallest event—was now terrifyingly real. The consequences of such actions were not just theoretical; they were tangible, destructive, and far-reaching. And if someone else managed to unlock the full potential of the Time Gate, they could undo everything—undo him, undo everything he had ever known.

"Where do we begin?" Ethan asked, his voice almost a whisper.

Lila stepped away from the stone throne and gestured for him to follow. She walked briskly toward the farthest corner of the room, where a large, ornate chest lay hidden beneath a draped cloth. The chest looked old—ancient, even—its wood weathered by time but still sturdy. The moment Lila's fingers brushed against the cloth, a hidden mechanism clicked, and the chest slowly creaked open, revealing an assortment of relics—scrolls, daggers, and worn leather-bound books, some of which appeared to glow faintly with a strange energy.

"This," Lila said softly, her hand hovering over the items, "is what's left of the city's greatest treasures. The knowledge of those who once lived here, who understood the true power of the Time Gate. These artifacts were created to protect the Gate, to control its power. But they were lost in the chaos that followed Darius's reign."

Ethan knelt beside her, his fingers brushing against one of the glowing scrolls. The symbols etched into its surface were unlike anything he had ever seen. They seemed to pulse with a rhythm, almost as if the scroll was alive, breathing in time with his own heartbeat.

"What do these symbols mean?" he asked, his voice barely above a whisper.

"They are the key to understanding the Time Gate's true purpose," Lila explained, her voice low and reverent. "The Gate itself isn't just a portal between time—it's a boundary, a threshold that separates the known world from the unknown. These artifacts were created by the original guardians of the city, who understood that the Gate's power could either be a boon or a curse. They believed that time should never be controlled or manipulated—it should be respected. The scrolls hold the knowledge of how to stabilize the Gate, how to prevent its power from being abused."

Ethan's eyes widened as he took in the weight of her words. The Time Gate was far more than just a tool—it was a delicate balance, a force that required immense respect and understanding. It was not meant to be wielded by just anyone, certainly not by someone like Darius, whose insatiable desire for power had led to the city's downfall.

"We need to find all the pieces," Ethan said, more to himself than to Lila. "We need to make sure no one else can get their hands on this knowledge."

Lila nodded, her eyes dark with determination. "Exactly. But we have to be careful. The Time Gate is a dangerous force, and those who seek to control it will stop at nothing to get what they want. We can't let history repeat itself. We need to find the pieces before they do, and we need to understand them fully—before it's too late."

As they stood there, the weight of their mission settling in, Ethan couldn't shake the feeling that they were being watched. The air seemed to grow heavier, the shadows darker. Something—or someone—was waiting for them to make their move. Ethan glanced over his shoulder, his senses on high alert. But there was nothing. Only the stillness of the ancient city, the echoes of a forgotten time.

Lila stood up, securing the scrolls and artifacts in a leather satchel. "We need to move quickly," she said, her voice resolute. "Every second counts. If Darius's legacy is going to be stopped, we need to stop it now."

Ethan nodded, his resolve hardening. The road ahead was dangerous, filled with uncertainty, but one thing was clear—he couldn't turn back now. Time itself was at stake.

ESCAPE AND PURSUIT

The weight of the ancient scrolls and relics pressed down on Ethan's shoulders as he and Lila hurried through the dimly lit hallways of the palace. The flickering torchlight cast eerie shadows on the walls, stretching and bending like ghostly figures, as though the very palace was watching them, aware of their every move. The air was thick with tension, and Ethan could feel his heartbeat thudding in his chest, louder than it should have been. Every footstep echoed in the silence, and he knew they didn't have much time.

Lila led the way, her pace swift and measured. Her eyes darted from side to side, scanning for any sign of danger. She had lived in this city her whole life, but Ethan could tell that even she was shaken by the events that had unfolded. The guards were closing in. Their plan to retrieve the relics had been uncovered far too quickly, and the king's soldiers, loyal to King Darius's unyielding desire to control time, were now on their trail.

"We need to move faster," Lila whispered urgently, her voice barely audible above the distant clamor of footsteps behind them. She pushed open a wooden door to their left, revealing a narrow corridor that led to the lower levels of the palace.

Ethan followed her without a word, his mind racing. He was still trying to process everything: the ancient power of the Time Gate, the legacy of King Darius, and now the reality that they were being hunted by the very guards meant to protect the kingdom. But there was no time for doubts. There was no time to wonder why Darius's followers were so determined to keep them from uncovering the truth. All that mattered now was survival.

The corridor was cold, damp, and lined with centuries-old stone. It was a stark contrast to the grandeur of the throne room, yet it offered a sense of safety, however temporary. They moved quickly, their footsteps muffled against the stone floor. Lila didn't slow down; she seemed to know exactly where she was going. Ethan trusted her instincts, but every now and then, he glanced over his shoulder, half-expecting to see the gleam of a sword or a shadow moving in the dark.

"Where are we going?" Ethan whispered, his voice strained.

"The underground tunnels," Lila replied, her eyes still ahead. "They were built long before the king's reign. They lead outside the city walls. If we can reach them, we'll be able to slip past the guards unnoticed."

Ethan nodded, though doubt gnawed at him. The tunnels were ancient, forgotten by most of the city's inhabitants. They were said to be vast and labyrinthine, winding beneath the ground in a maze of passages. While that made them perfect for escape, it also made them perilous. Who knew what dangers lurked in the forgotten corners of the palace?

They reached a large, iron-bound door at the end of the corridor. Lila pushed it open with a grunt, revealing a steep staircase leading down into the depths of the palace. The stairs were narrow and uneven, each step creaking under their weight. As they descended, the temperature seemed to drop, and Ethan could almost feel the walls closing in around him.

Suddenly, there was a loud crash behind them. The unmistakable sound of armored footsteps filled the hallway, growing louder with each passing second. The guards were closer than ever.

"They're here," Ethan hissed, panic rising in his chest. "Lila, we need to hurry!"

Lila's eyes widened, and she grabbed Ethan's arm, pulling him toward the bottom of the stairs. They reached the base of the staircase and turned a sharp corner into a long, narrow tunnel that stretched into the darkness. The air was thick with dust, and the sound of their breathing was the only thing that filled the silence.

"We're not safe yet," Lila said between breaths, her voice low and urgent. "They know these tunnels better than anyone. We'll have to move quickly and quietly. The moment they realize where we've gone, they'll be on our trail."

Ethan nodded grimly. He could hear the faint sounds of the guards' voices above them, shouting orders and searching the halls. They were on their way, and there was nowhere left to hide.

Lila led the way through the darkened tunnel, her movements fluid and quiet, like a shadow in the night. Ethan followed closely behind, doing his best to mimic her stealthy movements. The tunnel seemed to stretch on endlessly, twisting and turning, with no sign of an exit in sight.

Minutes felt like hours as they navigated the underground labyrinth. The only sound was the rhythmic echo of their footsteps, growing louder in the silence. Ethan's mind raced as he wondered if they were being led into a trap. He trusted Lila, but the walls felt like they were closing in.

Then, just as he was beginning to lose hope, Lila stopped abruptly, her hand shooting up in a signal to stop. Ethan froze, his heart skipping a beat.

"What is it?" he whispered, his breath coming out in quick bursts.

Lila pointed ahead. At the end of the tunnel, a faint light flickered in the distance, casting an eerie glow on the stone walls. It was the first sign of escape they had seen in what felt like forever. But it was too easy. Ethan's instincts screamed that something wasn't right.

Before he could voice his concern, the sound of footsteps echoed from the other end of the tunnel. They were closing in. The guards had found their trail. Ethan's pulse quickened. They were trapped. The light ahead was their only hope, but it could also be a trap.

"We have to move now," Lila urged, her voice tense. "Trust me."

Ethan didn't hesitate. They had no choice but to run.

They sprinted down the tunnel, the light growing brighter with each step. Behind them, the sounds of the guards' pursuit grew louder, their footsteps pounding on the stone like the drums of war. Ethan could hear their voices, shouting commands, but Lila's lead was unwavering.

As they reached the light, Ethan's heart skipped another beat. The tunnel opened into a vast chamber, an ancient cavern beneath the city, filled with the hum of energy and the faint flicker of glowing crystals embedded in the walls. The air was thick with a strange power, and Ethan could feel it vibrating through his very bones. This was no ordinary underground chamber. It felt like something out of a legend, a place forgotten by time.

But there was no time to admire the beauty. Lila pushed forward, weaving between jagged rocks and shimmering pools of water. They were almost there. Almost free.

Suddenly, a voice echoed through the chamber, sharp and commanding. "Stop! You're not getting away!"

The guards had caught up. Ethan glanced over his shoulder and saw several armored soldiers emerging from the tunnel, their faces hidden behind helmets. Their swords glinted menacingly in the dim light.

With a final burst of energy, Lila reached the edge of the cavern. Ahead of them lay a sheer drop—a chasm so deep it seemed to stretch into infinity. But it wasn't just the drop that made Ethan freeze. It was the portal, the glowing fissure in the air that pulsed like the heart of the universe itself. The Time Gate.

Lila turned to Ethan, her eyes filled with urgency. "We have no choice. We have to jump."

Ethan's breath caught in his throat as he looked down at the chasm below, the swirling energy of the Time Gate drawing him in with an almost magnetic force. It was their only chance.

Without another word, Lila leapt into the void. Ethan followed, his heart pounding, as the world around him dissolved into a blur of light and sound.

As Ethan followed Lila into the vast chasm, his mind raced with a mixture of terror and awe. The air around them shimmered with vibrant energy, the portal beckoning like an ancient, swirling vortex that defied the laws of physics. He could feel the gravitational pull intensifying as they descended, his limbs growing heavy and his surroundings becoming a blur of light. The noise of the world around him faded—no footsteps, no shouts from the guards. It was as if time itself had taken a breath, holding its collective anticipation.

For a split second, Ethan felt like they were suspended in nothingness. The world was a fluid mass of colors and whispers, too fast to comprehend yet too real to ignore. His heart was in his throat as the sensation of falling, not downward but outward, took over his body. It felt as though they were being stretched between moments in time. Then, with a sudden jolt, the chasm of light collapsed in on itself.

And then, everything stopped.

Ethan's feet slammed into solid ground, and he staggered, barely catching himself. The light around them dimmed to a dull glow, and the strange pull in his chest slowly faded. He blinked rapidly, trying to make sense of the disorienting transition.

They were no longer in the underground cavern. They were in a new place—a place that felt both distant and familiar.

Lila, however, was already on her feet, brushing dust from her cloak, her eyes scanning the surroundings with practiced caution. She didn't seem to share Ethan's shock, but then again, she had been through this before. She had known what to expect. Or at least, she thought she had.

The land around them stretched out in all directions—barren and desolate. The sky above was an unsettling shade of gray, with thick clouds swirling ominously, blocking any hint of sunlight.

The air had an unnatural stillness to it, as if the world itself was holding its breath. A chill seeped through Ethan's clothing, and he shivered involuntarily, his breath forming visible clouds in the cool atmosphere.

"What... where are we?" Ethan whispered, his voice still rattled from the chaotic leap through the portal. The questions rushed to his mind faster than he could process them. What had just happened? Had they left the ancient city entirely, or had the Time Gate taken them to a different point in time—or even a parallel world?

"This is... I don't know exactly," Lila murmured, her tone uncertain. "I didn't expect this place."

Ethan frowned, scanning the barren horizon. It felt like an abandoned world, a place forgotten by time, or perhaps a time that had never been. The terrain before them was jagged, with dark mountains in the far distance, their peaks obscured by swirling mist. There was no sign of life—no animals, no birds, nothing to indicate that this was a living world at all. The ground beneath their feet was cracked and dry, and in places, strange glowing cracks ran along the surface like veins, pulsing with an eerie, otherworldly light.

"This isn't normal," Lila continued, her voice low but firm. "This place... it's not part of the usual pathways the Time Gate leads to. We've ended up somewhere outside of time, or in a time that shouldn't exist."

Ethan's thoughts raced. He tried to piece together what he knew about time travel. The Time Gate, as powerful as it was, was supposed to open doors to various points in time—both past and future. But this place didn't fit the description of anything he had imagined. It was as though they had slipped between the cracks of time itself and found themselves in a limbo, a place that shouldn't exist, a place where the rules of time and space were suspended.

"How do we get out?" Ethan asked, his voice trembling slightly despite himself.

Lila turned to him, her expression one of quiet resolve. "We don't," she replied, a hint of dread creeping into her voice. "At least, not easily. We need to figure out what this place is first—why the Time

Gate brought us here. And then, we need to find another portal, another gateway to escape."

Ethan nodded, though a sense of unease settled in his stomach. If there was no clear way out, what were they supposed to do? Survive? Wait for another portal to open? The uncertainty gnawed at him. But there was no choice. They had to press on, no matter how strange and unsettling this new place was.

Lila motioned for him to follow, and without another word, they began to walk across the desolate land. Each step seemed to echo unnervingly loud, and the silence around them was deafening. There was no sign of the king's guards, but Ethan couldn't shake the feeling that they were still being watched. Even in this strange, timeless place, he couldn't escape the weight of the pursuit.

As they walked, the oddities of the place became more apparent. The ground was littered with ancient, crumbling structures—what looked like the remnants of an old civilization, perhaps one that had fallen long ago. Ruined temples and broken statues were scattered across the landscape, half-buried under the dry earth. Some of the statues were of figures Ethan didn't recognize, their faces worn by the passage of time, their features almost otherworldly. There were signs of former life here, but they were all lifeless now. It was as if everything in this place had been abandoned, left to wither in the void between time.

And yet, there was something familiar about the statues. Ethan couldn't quite place it, but there was a sensation of déjà vu, as though he had seen them before in some distant dream or forgotten memory. His thoughts spiraled as he struggled to recall where he had seen them—then, the realization struck him. The figures in the statues bore a striking resemblance to King Darius himself.

"What is this place?" Ethan murmured, more to himself than to Lila. "These statues... they look like Darius."

Lila stopped walking for a moment, her expression growing darker as she studied the ruins around them. "I don't think we're in any normal place, Ethan. It's as if this place… this time… is tied to Darius's past. But not the past we know. This is something older. Something far more dangerous."

Her words hung in the air, and Ethan felt a chill run down his spine. He had come to understand that time was a powerful force, one that could warp and change things in unimaginable ways. But what if Darius's desire for control over time had gone too far? What if they were standing on the precipice of something even more catastrophic than they realized?

As the silence stretched between them, Ethan realized that the journey ahead would be far more complicated than he could have ever expected. And as they ventured deeper into the unknown, there was one thing he knew for certain: they weren't just running from the king anymore. They were running from time itself.

With the soldiers' footsteps growing fainter in the distance, Ethan and Lila hurried through the winding alleys of the ancient city. The weight of their escape pressed heavily on their shoulders, but they didn't have time to slow down. Every corner they turned seemed more labyrinthine, more claustrophobic—like the city itself was trying to trap them.

Lila's breath came in short bursts, and Ethan's heart pounded like a war drum in his chest. They had to move quickly. The king's guards were relentless, and the longer they stayed in one place, the more likely they were to be found. They couldn't afford that. Not with what they had learned.

Ethan glanced over at Lila, her face pale, but determined. Her eyes were fixed on the distant horizon, her steps quick and purposeful. He could tell she had been through this before, but there was a new urgency in her movements—an unease that hadn't been there when they first started this journey together. Ethan couldn't help but wonder what she was keeping from him, what secrets lay buried behind her stoic expression.

"Lila, wait," Ethan called softly, pulling her arm to slow her down. He wanted to ask more about the Time Gate, about where they were headed, but he could sense she was trying to keep her mind focused on the immediate threat.

"We can't stop here, Ethan," she said, voice low and tense. "We don't have much time before they realize we've gone. The city's pathways are riddled with traps—one wrong move, and we could be caught in one."

Ethan nodded, the gravity of her words settling in his chest. He had no idea what dangers lurked in the city's shadows, but he knew they had to get out—fast. They didn't have a plan. They didn't even know where they were headed. All they knew was that if they stayed still for too long, the king's forces would catch up with them—and when they did, there would be no escape.

They took another turn, deeper into the maze of streets. The architecture here was unlike anything Ethan had ever seen, with towering structures that seemed to defy logic—large spirals reaching toward the sky, walls etched with symbols that shimmered faintly in the twilight. It was as if the city itself was alive, breathing with ancient power.

But their escape wouldn't be easy.

Suddenly, a loud crash echoed from the distance, followed by a shout. Ethan's blood froze. The guards had found their trail. They were getting closer.

Lila grabbed his wrist and yanked him toward an open doorway ahead. "Through here!" she hissed, pulling him into a shadowed corridor. The door slammed shut behind them, sealing them in darkness. They were now in the bowels of the city, a network of narrow, underground tunnels where the echoes of footsteps above felt distant, almost unreal.

Inside, the air was thick with dust, and the smell of ancient stone mixed with something metallic—perhaps the remnants of a forgotten civilization. Ethan's eyes took a moment to adjust to the dim light filtering in from small cracks in the walls. The silence was oppressive, each footfall seeming to vibrate through the ground beneath them.

"Where are we going, Lila?" Ethan asked, his voice barely above a whisper.

Lila didn't answer right away. She was scanning the tunnels, her brow furrowed in concentration. She was trying to figure out their next move, and time was running out. The sound of distant voices and the metallic clatter of guards' armor filled the air, growing louder as the seconds passed. They couldn't stay hidden forever.

Ethan felt the weight of the situation on his shoulders. They were in a race against time—quite literally—and the clock was ticking down.

"There's a place," Lila said finally, her voice trembling just slightly. "An old hidden chamber deep beneath the city. It's the only place they won't think to look for us. But we have to move fast. If we're caught, we won't make it out alive."

Ethan swallowed hard. The urgency in her voice was unmistakable. They had to trust each other now, or they wouldn't stand a chance.

Without another word, they plunged deeper into the underground labyrinth. The walls closed in on them as they navigated the narrow corridors, their footsteps soft but hurried. They passed doors, archways, and passageways that seemed to stretch on endlessly, each one offering more potential escape routes but also leading them deeper into unknown dangers. There was no clear map to this place, no reliable path that could guarantee their safety. Each turn was a gamble, each decision a risk.

But they had no choice.

As they rounded yet another corner, Ethan felt his pulse quicken. He could hear the guards now—too close. Their voices were sharper, more insistent, and their search was growing more frantic. Ethan's heart thudded in his chest. They had to find the chamber before the guards found them.

Then, just as Ethan thought they were trapped, Lila stopped abruptly. In front of them was a large stone door, partially hidden by ivy and debris. It looked ancient, worn with time, but it stood firm, solid—a possible escape.

"This is it," Lila said breathlessly, moving toward the door. She pressed her hand against the stone, her fingers tracing an intricate pattern that ran across the surface. Slowly, almost ceremoniously, the door creaked open, revealing a darkened room beyond.

Ethan followed her inside, and they quickly closed the door behind them. They were safe—for now.

Inside the chamber, the air was cooler, and the oppressive weight of the outside world seemed to lift, replaced by a strange tranquility. The room was surprisingly simple—a stone floor, a few forgotten relics scattered around, and strange markings etched into the walls. But it felt different from everything else in the city. It was as if this chamber had been forgotten by time itself, untouched by the hands of the guards and the tyranny of King Darius.

Lila turned to Ethan, her face grim. "We may have bought ourselves some time, but the danger is far from over. Darius isn't going to stop until he has what he wants. We've only just begun to unravel the secrets of this city... and I fear that the truth we're about to uncover will be even more dangerous than we could ever imagine."

Ethan looked at her, his resolve hardening. He knew this was only the beginning. Whatever lay ahead—whatever dangers awaited them in the dark recesses of this city—they would face it together. They had no other choice.

A JOURNEY FOR HOPE

The chamber's oppressive stillness felt like a silent warning, urging Ethan and Lila to leave before they were discovered. But for now, they were safe—protected by the thick stone walls of their temporary refuge. Lila sat against the cool, moss-covered stone, her brow furrowed as she pondered their next move. Ethan, pacing slowly across the room, couldn't shake the gnawing sense of urgency that tugged at him. The king's relentless pursuit was not just about capture—it was about control. Time itself was at stake.

For a brief moment, their world outside felt like another reality—one of endless dangers and uncertainty. Yet, in this forgotten chamber, time seemed to stand still, as though the very walls were holding their breath.

Ethan couldn't stop thinking about the consequences of King Darius's plan. The king wasn't just after power over the city—he sought dominion over time itself. A king who could manipulate the fabric of time would not only conquer the past and the future but would reshape everything in his image, erasing history, distorting reality, and wielding unimaginable destruction. They had to stop him before it was too late. But how?

Lila finally broke the silence. Her voice was soft but determined, a quiet strength emanating from her as she spoke. "We can't stay here forever, Ethan. Darius's soldiers are relentless, and sooner or later, they'll find us. But there's a way we can stop him—a way we can unravel the power he seeks to control."

Ethan turned to face her, eyes wide with curiosity. "You know how to stop him?"

Lila nodded, standing up and brushing the dust from her clothes. "Yes. But it won't be easy. There's a place, far beyond the city, where the ancient artifacts that power the Time Gate are hidden. They are the key to controlling the flow of time—if we can reach them before Darius does."

The gravity of her words hit Ethan like a punch to the gut. A part of him wanted to question her—demand more information—but deep down, he knew she wasn't lying. He could see the conviction in her eyes, the weight of a burden far too heavy for anyone so young to carry. It was a truth she had been carrying for a long time, a truth she couldn't avoid any longer.

"You're telling me the artifacts are the only way to stop Darius?" Ethan asked, his voice shaking slightly from the weight of his realization.

Lila's gaze turned to the floor for a moment, as if the weight of their task was overwhelming even her. "Yes. The artifacts are scattered across different locations—places hidden away from the prying eyes of the world. Only those with a deep understanding of the ancient knowledge can find them. And only together, with the right balance of courage, intelligence, and heart, can we use them to undo what Darius plans to do."

Ethan swallowed hard, feeling the enormity of their task pressing down on him. "How do we even begin? We're just two people—how can we take on the most powerful king in history?"

Lila smiled faintly, a glimmer of hope in her eyes. "Because we're not alone, Ethan. The world is filled with secrets, and in the shadows of time, there are those who still fight against tyranny. If we find the right people, we can gather allies who will help us. We just have to trust in each other, and in what we believe is right."

Ethan felt a surge of determination. Despite the fear gnawing at his insides, he felt something else—hope. A flicker of hope that perhaps, together, they could change the course of history.

Without another word, they stood side by side, preparing for the journey ahead. They didn't have all the answers, and the road would be fraught with danger, but they had each other. And that, for the moment, was enough.

As they stepped out of the hidden chamber, the cool night air greeted them like a silent promise. The city of the past sprawled before them, ancient streets stretching out in all directions. Ethan looked at Lila, waiting for her to lead the way. She didn't hesitate. With a steady pace, she took the lead, her eyes scanning the horizon, looking for any signs of the path that lay before them.

Ethan's mind raced as they moved through the shadowed streets. He could feel the weight of their mission like a chain wrapped around his chest. The stakes had never been higher, and every moment they spent in the city was a moment they were closer to being caught. Yet, he couldn't help but feel a strange sense of excitement. They were on the cusp of something extraordinary—something that could change the world forever.

"Where are we going?" Ethan finally asked, his voice breaking through the silence of their journey.

Lila glanced over her shoulder. "We need to find the First Artifact," she said, her voice steady but tinged with urgency. "It's hidden in a temple, deep within the Forest of Echoes. But getting there won't be easy. We'll need to cross dangerous lands, avoid Darius's patrols, and uncover clues that have been buried for centuries."

The Forest of Echoes. Ethan had heard of it. A place of legends, where the trees whispered secrets of the past, and the air was thick with magic. It sounded like something out of a dream—or a nightmare. But there was no turning back now.

Lila quickened her pace. "Come on. We don't have much time. The longer we wait, the closer Darius gets to unraveling the Time Gate and reshaping the world."

Ethan nodded, his heart pounding in his chest. Every step forward was a step into the unknown, and the weight of their mission bore down on him like a storm. But there was no turning back now. He had made his choice, and he would fight for the future—whatever the cost.

As they ventured deeper into the shadows of the city, their path uncertain but their resolve unshaken, Ethan couldn't help but wonder about the artifacts. What kind of power did they hold? Could they really stop a man as powerful as King Darius? And what about the allies Lila mentioned—would they be enough to tip the balance in their favor?

Only time would tell. And with each passing moment, they drew closer to the Forest of Echoes—and to the hope that it contained.

The moonlight filtered through the ancient city's crumbling rooftops, casting long shadows along the narrow streets. Ethan and Lila moved quietly, their footsteps almost muffled by the soft dust beneath them. The weight of their journey hung heavily in the air, and with every step they took, the tension between them grew. They were heading toward the Forest of Echoes—a place of whispers and forgotten memories, where the first of the ancient artifacts was said to be hidden.

But there was a sense of dread that lingered in the air, like an invisible hand reaching out, pulling them deeper into the unknown. Ethan had been to forests before, but none like this. The legends told of trees that could speak, that listened to the past and foresaw the future. The air, thick with ancient magic, was both welcoming and foreboding. He couldn't shake the feeling that the forest itself would watch them, waiting for them to uncover its secrets—or perish in the attempt.

Lila had heard those same stories. She walked with purpose, her gaze fixed ahead, but Ethan could see the flicker of uncertainty in her eyes. She had heard the warnings. The Forest of Echoes wasn't a place for the faint of heart. Yet, she remained resolute, as if the weight of their mission had forged an unbreakable resolve within her.

The night was cold, but not unbearably so. Still, Ethan shivered, his breath coming in short bursts. The city they had escaped from seemed to close in behind them, as though it were swallowing their steps. The sense of pursuit had not abated; they were being hunted. Every alley they passed, every street corner, felt like it held a watchful eye.

As they neared the outskirts of the city, Lila stopped, turning to Ethan with a serious expression. "We'll be entering the forest soon," she said, her voice low. "You must understand the dangers we face. The forest isn't just alive with magic—it has a mind of its own. It will test us, challenge us, and it won't hesitate to send us into illusions if we're not careful."

Ethan nodded, but his mind raced. "How do we know we're not already in one of its illusions? How can we trust anything we see or hear?"

Lila gave him a sad smile. "That's the hardest part of the journey. The forest doesn't reveal its truth easily. We'll need to trust each other and the path we choose, even if the forest tries to trick us."

With a deep breath, Ethan followed Lila as she led them to the edge of the forest. The towering trees seemed to loom ahead, their gnarled branches twisting in unnatural shapes, as if reaching down to snatch them up. The air here felt different—thicker, heavier. A soft wind stirred the leaves, and Ethan thought he heard faint whispers carried on the breeze. It was as though the forest itself was alive, waiting.

The forest was rumored to be more than just a mystical place—it was said to be a living entity that had seen the rise and fall of countless kingdoms. Some believed that the forest was the birthplace of time itself, a place where the natural flow of time could be bent, distorted, and even rewritten. It was a place of ancient power, where only those who were chosen could uncover its secrets.

"Stay close," Lila whispered, as she led them deeper into the trees. "The forest has a way of disorienting you. The deeper we go, the more difficult it will be to stay on the right path."

Ethan felt a knot of fear form in his stomach, but he pushed it down. They couldn't afford to lose their resolve now. Not when they were so close to stopping Darius.

As they ventured further into the forest, the sounds of the outside world faded. The only noise was the occasional rustle of leaves underfoot, the creak of trees in the wind, and the whispers of the forest itself. Ethan's senses were on high alert. Every snap of a twig, every shifting shadow made his heart race. The forest seemed to be shifting around them, as if the path ahead was constantly changing, leading them deeper into the unknown.

Lila, who had been walking in front, suddenly stopped, holding up a hand. Ethan immediately tensed, his hand instinctively reaching for the knife at his side.

"Do you hear that?" Lila asked, her voice barely above a whisper.

Ethan strained his ears, trying to pick up any sound beyond the rustling of the leaves. At first, he heard nothing. But then, in the distance, a faint, rhythmic thudding noise broke through the silence—a sound like footsteps. Heavy, deliberate footsteps.

Lila's eyes narrowed. "It's him," she muttered under her breath. "King Darius's men are here."

Panic surged through Ethan's chest. They had been too slow. The soldiers had found them. But before he could voice his concern, Lila grabbed his arm, pulling him toward a large, gnarled tree with a hollow at its base.

"Quick!" she whispered. "We need to hide. If they see us, we're done for."

Without hesitation, Ethan followed her, crouching low as they both slipped into the hollow. The air inside was cooler, and the dense wood of the tree trunk created a tight, confined space. They barely had time to catch their breath before the footsteps grew louder, closer. The soldiers were drawing near.

Ethan's heart raced, his pulse pounding in his ears. He felt trapped, helpless, as the heavy footsteps continued, passing by their hiding place. Through the crack in the tree's bark, Ethan could see the dim outlines of the soldiers—clad in the heavy armor of King Darius's elite guard. They were searching for them, their weapons gleaming in the low light.

Lila's grip tightened on Ethan's arm. "Stay still," she whispered urgently.

For what felt like an eternity, they remained motionless, the soldiers continuing their search. Ethan could feel his muscles stiffening, the weight of the moment pressing down on him. His mind raced with thoughts of how to escape, how to outsmart these soldiers. But the forest was their ally, and perhaps it would offer them a chance. They just had to wait for the right moment.

The footsteps eventually grew fainter, and with a final glance in their direction, the soldiers moved on. Lila let out a quiet sigh of relief. Ethan's heart was still racing, but he knew they couldn't stay hidden forever. They had to keep moving—keep pushing forward.

Lila took a deep breath and stood. "We're not safe yet. But we're one step closer."

Ethan nodded, his determination growing stronger. They would make it through this. They had to. There was no turning back now.

As they ventured further into the depths of the Forest of Echoes, the air thick with tension, they had no idea what awaited them. The path ahead was fraught with dangers and uncertainties, but with each step,

Ethan felt the weight of their mission become clearer. They weren't just fighting for their own survival—they were fighting for the future of time itself.

The dense canopy of the Forest of Echoes stretched above them, a thick tangle of branches and leaves that seemed to close in with every step. Despite the occasional rustle of the wind and the distant hoot of an owl, the silence of the forest was suffocating. It felt like an unseen force pressed in around them, its weight so tangible that Ethan could almost hear the forest's ancient whispers urging him forward, yet warning him to turn back.

Ethan's thoughts were consumed with one thing: stopping King Darius. The gravity of their mission weighed heavily on his chest, each step reminding him of the destructive power the king sought to control. Darius wasn't just after land or riches—he sought the very flow of time itself, to bend it to his will. And if he succeeded, it would not just change the course of history—it could unravel everything Ethan had ever known. The thought of such power falling into the wrong hands left a bitter taste in his mouth.

The path they walked seemed endless, each tree, each bend in the trail looking identical to the last. Ethan's sense of time had already been distorted—how long had they been walking? Minutes? Hours? The dense fog had thickened, clouding their vision, making it harder to see the way ahead. They had no map, no clear directions—just the vague promise of ancient knowledge hidden deep within the forest.

Lila walked ahead, her posture rigid, scanning the path ahead. Her face was set in determination, but Ethan could sense the undercurrent of worry beneath her calm exterior. She had been in the forest before, but never under such dire circumstances. This time, they weren't just looking for an artifact or a safe haven—they were racing against a king who wielded dark magic and an army of merciless soldiers.

"How much farther?" Ethan asked quietly, trying to keep his voice steady. His legs were beginning to ache, and the oppressive silence of the forest made it hard to focus.

Lila glanced back at him, her brow furrowed. "I can't say for certain. The forest changes, shifts. You can walk for hours, only to find yourself in the same place. But don't worry. We'll reach the Clearing of Time soon. It's the last known location of the artifact."

Ethan nodded, though a part of him was unsure whether he should believe her. Could this forest really be that deceptive? Was there truly a way out—or was it all just an illusion, a trick of the forest's magic?

As if to answer his question, the ground suddenly trembled beneath their feet. The trees around them seemed to groan, and a gust of wind whipped through the forest, rustling the leaves in an eerie chorus. The path ahead blurred, and Ethan's vision became momentarily distorted, as though the world itself was bending, warping in front of his eyes.

"What was that?" Ethan asked, his voice a whisper, as if speaking too loudly might shatter the fragile moment.

Lila's eyes widened, her expression one of deep concern. "It's the forest. It's trying to test us." Her voice dropped lower, a hint of fear creeping into it.

"We have to keep moving. If we stop here, we could get lost forever."

Suddenly, from the corner of his eye, Ethan thought he saw a figure in the distance—a shadow flickering between the trees. It was only for a moment, but the figure was unmistakable, moving swiftly, as if it knew exactly where it was going.

"Did you see that?" Ethan asked, his heart pounding in his chest. "There was something over there. Someone."

Lila didn't answer immediately. She was too busy staring at the same spot. Ethan could see her fists clenched at her sides, her body tense, every muscle in her body poised for action.

"I don't know," she finally whispered, "but we can't afford to let it distract us. Stay close."

They quickened their pace, the eerie silence of the forest broken only by the sound of their hurried footsteps. The whispering trees seemed to follow their every movement, their long branches creaking and bending as though they were alive, watching them.

As they moved deeper into the forest, Ethan began to feel the forest's grip tightening around them. The further they went, the more the air seemed to thicken, heavy with the weight of forgotten memories and ancient secrets. It was as if the forest was actively resisting them, testing their resolve with every step.

"I think we're close," Lila said, her voice barely audible above the growing winds. "But we have to hurry."

Before Ethan could respond, the ground beneath them began to shift once more. The path split into two, the options equally dark and foreboding. One trail was bathed in a pale, ghostly light, while the other was completely shrouded in darkness. Ethan's heart raced as he looked between the two paths, torn.

"The Clearing of Time lies at the end of the path on the left," Lila said, her voice steady despite the growing tension. "But this is where the forest's illusions are the strongest. We must be careful."

The air seemed to crackle with energy as the trees around them began to sway violently, and the forest grew louder with the sound of unseen creatures and whispering voices. Ethan felt his head spinning, his thoughts fragmented. He reached for Lila's hand, his fingers brushing hers as they stepped onto the path leading into the pale light.

As they continued on their journey, the path seemed to stretch impossibly long. Each step felt like they were moving deeper into the heart of the forest's power. The farther they went, the more distorted the world became. The trees shifted before their eyes, the shapes of the shadows twisting into grotesque forms, and the whispers grew louder, rising to a crescendo that echoed in their minds.

They had to trust the forest, trust that the path they were on would lead them to their destination. Time was running out.

Just as Ethan thought he might collapse under the pressure, the path before them suddenly opened into a clearing—a vast, open space that seemed untouched by time itself. In the center stood a tall, ancient tree, its bark gleaming with an ethereal glow, surrounded by a circle of stones, each one inscribed with ancient runes.

"This is it," Lila said, her voice filled with awe. "The Clearing of Time. The artifact is somewhere here."

Ethan stood frozen, his breath caught in his throat. The silence that had once gripped the forest was now replaced by an intense, palpable energy. The Clearing of Time was real—it existed, just as the legends had promised. And now, standing in its presence, Ethan realized that this moment was not just a chance to stop King Darius. It was their only chance to prevent the collapse of everything he knew.

THE KEY TO TIME

Ethan stood frozen, his gaze fixed on the ancient tree in the center of the Clearing of Time. The tree's bark shimmered with a subtle, otherworldly glow, and the air around it seemed thick with power—an almost tangible energy that hummed and thrummed against his skin. As he took a step forward, the silence of the forest seemed to fall into a deeper hush, as though the very space around him was holding its breath.

Lila stood beside him, her eyes scanning the clearing with cautious optimism. "This is it, Ethan. This is where everything changes. We're so close."

Ethan's heart pounded in his chest as he surveyed the mystical circle of stones, each one intricately inscribed with symbols that seemed to move and shift when he looked at them for too long. The path that had brought them here felt like a blur now, every step taken in haste, every moment on edge. But now, standing in the Clearing of Time, everything around him seemed to slow, as though the world was finally pausing to acknowledge their arrival.

His hand instinctively reached for his pocket watch. He hadn't given it much thought since the beginning of their journey. The watch had been a family heirloom passed down from generations, its ticking barely audible but ever-present. But now, as his fingers brushed its cold surface, something stirred within him—an undeniable sense of purpose, of connection.

He pulled the watch out, his thumb grazing the polished surface. For a brief moment, the world around him flickered, like a camera lens out of focus. The symbols on the stones shifted again, their movements becoming more defined, more deliberate. Ethan's breath caught in his throat as the watch began to glow faintly in his hand, its golden surface pulsing with the rhythm of his heartbeat.

"It's… it's doing something," Ethan whispered, as though speaking too loudly would break the fragile magic in the air. The soft hum of energy in the clearing seemed to respond to his words, vibrating with increased intensity.

Lila turned to face him, her expression a mixture of confusion and awe. "What is happening? Ethan, why is your watch glowing?"

Ethan's mind raced. He had felt it before—when he first held the watch as a child, the same strange pull. The watch had always been special, but until now, he had never understood its true significance. It had never glowed like this, never carried the weight of the forest's magic. But in this moment, in this place, everything was different. The forest seemed to recognize the watch's power, as if it had been waiting for this very moment.

He stared at the watch intently, as though searching for answers in its intricate design. There was something about the way the gears clicked and turned, something ancient embedded deep within its mechanism. The watch was more than a mere timepiece—it was a key. But a key to what?

"I don't understand…" Ethan muttered, his voice barely above a whisper.

Lila's voice interrupted his thoughts, steady but filled with wonder. "Maybe it's not just a watch, Ethan. Maybe it's a part of the artifact. The stories

I've heard—they spoke of an ancient artifact that could control time. Could this watch be it?"

Ethan blinked, his mind racing. "You mean... my watch is the artifact?"

Lila nodded slowly, her eyes never leaving the glowing object in his hand. "It's possible. This place, this clearing, is a nexus of time. Everything here exists outside the bounds of ordinary time—past, present, and future all converge in this spot. And the watch… it's the key that can unlock that power."

Ethan's grip tightened around the watch as the realization settled over him. It wasn't just a family heirloom. It wasn't just something passed down through generations. The watch was the key to unlocking everything. Time itself. The forest. The future. And most importantly, it was the key to stopping King Darius.

For the first time in their journey, Ethan felt a flicker of hope. The odds had seemed insurmountable. The weight of their mission had been unbearable at times. But now, with the power of the watch in his hand, he could sense a way forward. A way to change everything.

As the glow from the watch intensified, a sharp, piercing sound broke through the stillness—the faintest sound of ticking, but unlike any tick Ethan had ever heard before. The sound echoed through the clearing, growing louder and louder, until it was impossible to ignore. The stones surrounding them seemed to pulse in time with the ticking, their runes becoming clearer, more defined, until they resembled something entirely different—a map, a pathway.

Lila stepped closer, her voice filled with awe. "Ethan, look! The symbols—they're forming something. It's like they're… guiding us."

Ethan stared in disbelief. The symbols on the stones were no longer just abstract shapes; they had begun to form a pattern, an intricate web of connections that spanned the entire clearing. The watch was the catalyst, unlocking the hidden structure beneath the surface of the forest. And in the center, where the energy seemed to converge, Ethan saw a new symbol emerge—a symbol that looked familiar, yet entirely alien. A circle with an eye in the center, radiating lines that stretched out to the edge of the clearing.

The vision before him made his heart race with a new sense of urgency. "It's showing us the way. This is the path to stopping Darius."

Lila's voice was barely a whisper. "Then what are we waiting for?"

Ethan knew that they had to act now. They had come so far, faced so many trials, and now the truth was within their grasp. The watch wasn't just a key to the forest—it was the key to everything. If they could harness its power, they could stop King Darius before he ever got the chance to rewrite time itself.

The glowing watch pulsed once more, sending a ripple through the air, and then, as if responding to an unseen command, the path revealed itself fully before them. It was a narrow corridor of energy, vibrating with the raw power of time itself, leading deeper into the forest. But as Ethan took a step forward, the ground trembled once more, this time more violently, and a dark shadow loomed on the horizon.

King Darius was closer than they realized.

Ethan felt his pulse quicken as he stared at the glowing path stretching out before them. The corridor of energy hummed with an ancient power, vibrating with each heartbeat as though the very fabric of time itself was alive. The air around him was thick, almost electric, as the watch in his hand began to heat up. The golden casing was warm to the touch, the familiar tick of its mechanism now a constant, steady rhythm, but strangely it felt more like a heartbeat—alive, connected to the forest and everything around them.

Lila's eyes gleamed with a mixture of awe and apprehension. "This... this is it, isn't it? The way forward?"

Ethan could hardly believe what he was seeing. The path, now clearly visible before them, was a narrow thread of shifting light, stretching deeper into the forest as though it had always been there, waiting for them to find it. The energy pulsed with such force that the air seemed to tremble, and the trees surrounding the clearing swayed as though bowing in reverence to the power emanating from the heart of the forest. It was as if time itself had cracked open, revealing a secret long kept hidden, waiting for the right person to unlock it.

He stepped forward, his feet crunching softly against the underbrush, and immediately the ground seemed to shift beneath him. The light of the path flickered, and for the briefest moment, Ethan felt a sharp pull—like gravity was bending, twisting around him. His senses were overwhelmed, a feeling of vertigo sweeping over him as if he were standing on the edge of something vast, something beyond his understanding.

"Are you sure we're ready for this?" Lila asked, her voice low, filled with uncertainty. Her brow was furrowed in concern, her eyes never leaving the glowing path. "What if we're walking into something we can't control?"

Ethan didn't have an answer, at least not one that would reassure her. He didn't fully understand what they were about to do, but one thing was certain: the watch had brought them this far, and it held the key to everything. It was their only chance to stop King Darius before his plans for time manipulation consumed the entire world.

"I think we have no choice," Ethan said, his voice steady despite the storm of emotions whirling within him. "This watch is the only thing that can stop him. If we don't take this path, we risk losing everything."

With a deep breath, Lila nodded. She could sense the urgency in Ethan's voice, and though she still had her doubts, she trusted him. Together, they had already faced so much. Now, they were on the precipice of something far greater than either of them could have ever imagined.

Ethan stepped onto the path. The instant his foot touched the first flickering light, he felt an overwhelming surge of energy course through him. It was as though the very essence of time itself flowed into his body, filling him with knowledge — knowledge of things he couldn't possibly understand. His vision blurred, and he stumbled, his hand gripping the pocket watch tighter as if it were anchoring him to reality. But despite the confusion that threatened to overtake him, Ethan knew one thing for certain: he had to keep moving forward.

The light around them began to grow brighter, enveloping them both in a dazzling glow. Ethan could barely make out the trees and the world around him as the path grew ever more intense, pulling them deeper into the unknown. The rhythm of the watch's ticking seemed to sync with his heartbeat, steadying his breath, grounding him to the moment.

At that very moment, a voice echoed in his mind—clear and sharp, like a whisper carried on the wind.

The key to time lies within, but only the worthy shall wield its power.

The words reverberated within Ethan's chest, sending a chill down his spine. He stopped, momentarily overwhelmed by the sheer weight of what he had just heard. The voice wasn't Lila's—it wasn't from the clearing. It was ancient, almost primordial in its tone.

Lila noticed his sudden stillness and stepped closer. "Ethan? What is it?"

Ethan shook his head, blinking rapidly. "Did you hear that? A voice... It said something about being worthy."

Lila's brow furrowed in confusion, but she didn't question him. "We need to keep moving. I don't know what that was, but we don't have time to figure it out right now."

They pressed forward, the shimmering path pulling them along as though the forest itself were guiding their steps. The deeper they ventured, the more Ethan felt that familiar pull from the watch—this time, more intense than before. His hand gripped the watch harder as he felt a sudden pull toward an invisible force ahead.

Ahead, in the distance, the light from the path intensified, and Ethan realized that they were nearing the heart of the forest. The air grew thicker, heavier with magic, and he could feel the weight of countless ages pressing down on him. The clearing behind them now felt like a distant memory, the outside world slipping further away as they stepped closer to the unknown.

Then, as if answering their silent question, the path split into two. One path veered off to the left, dark and foreboding, while the other continued straight ahead, bathed in blinding light. The energy from the watch pulsed stronger as Ethan's gaze shifted between the two, trying to make sense of the choice before them.

"We have to choose," Lila said, her voice calm but heavy with uncertainty. "Which path leads to the heart of time? Which one will give us the power we need to stop King Darius?"

Ethan stared at the paths, his mind racing. He could feel the pressure of the moment, the weight of destiny bearing down on him. The voice, the ancient warning—it was all coming together. This wasn't just about stopping Darius; it was about understanding time, about unlocking something far greater than either of them had anticipated.

He could feel the pull from both paths—the dark one and the one bathed in light. They both led forward, but in different ways. One promised knowledge, but at a cost. The other was uncertain, filled with the unknown.

"Ethan," Lila urged, "we can't waste time. The king is getting closer. We have to decide."

Ethan nodded slowly, his grip tightening around the watch. He took a deep breath, feeling the ancient power coursing through him. The decision weighed heavily on him, but he could feel something inside — a quiet certainty.

"Light," he murmured, his voice steady with newfound resolve. "We have to trust the light."

Without another word, he stepped toward the path of light, feeling the energy intensify as they walked forward. The ground trembled beneath them, and the air hummed with the power of time itself, but Ethan didn't look back. This was their only chance. There was no turning back now.

As they continued down the radiant path, the light grew blinding, and the space around them began to warp and twist. Ethan's heart raced, the pocket watch vibrating violently in his hand. They were nearing the core of time — and whatever waited there, they would have to face it together.

As Ethan and Lila made their way deeper into the shimmering light, they felt as though the very air around them had shifted. It was no longer just the forest surrounding them, but something much larger, something beyond the comprehension of their senses. The light from the path was blinding, overwhelming in its brilliance. Every step seemed to bring them closer to the heart of time itself, a place where reality felt unstable, as though the laws of physics, logic, and time itself were bending and folding around them.

Ethan's mind raced. The watch in his hand had never felt more alive. He could feel it pulsating in rhythm with his heart, its once quiet ticking now resonating in the air around them, magnified into a low hum that vibrated through his bones. It was as if the watch was no longer just a tool, but the key to unlocking something far greater than time—perhaps the very fabric of the universe itself.

"What is this place?" Lila asked, her voice barely audible over the overwhelming hum. "It feels like we're walking inside time itself."

Ethan didn't answer at first. He didn't have the words. The path ahead stretched endlessly, and the more they walked, the more it seemed as though the world around them was shifting. The trees that had once lined the edge of the path were now distant echoes, their silhouettes fading into the glow. The ground beneath their feet seemed to pulse, as though it were breathing, as though the earth itself was alive and aware of their presence.

The air grew colder, and a soft breeze swept through, carrying with it an ancient, almost imperceptible whisper. It was a voice—a low, gentle murmur that seemed to be calling to Ethan from the depths of the path.

The watch is not just an object, the voice whispered, *It is the vessel. The vessel for your choices. What you decide now will shape the course of time.*

Ethan stopped in his tracks, the words echoing in his mind. The voice wasn't from the watch—it was something else. A presence, perhaps. A force beyond the world they knew. He looked down at the watch in his hand, still pulsing with energy, its surface glimmering with an iridescent sheen that made it appear almost otherworldly.

Lila looked at him, sensing the shift in his demeanor. "Ethan, what's happening? What did you hear?"

He took a deep breath and exhaled slowly. "It's telling me that the watch is more than just a timepiece. It's the key to something much larger. A vessel for the choices we're about to make."

She nodded, understanding the gravity of the situation, though uncertainty still clouded her features. "What do we do with that knowledge?"

Before he could respond, the light ahead of them began to distort, swirling like a vortex. The path beneath their feet seemed to ripple, and the ground itself began to tremble. The sensation was both terrifying and exhilarating, as though the very essence of time was bending around them. The watch in his hand grew hotter, the pulse more insistent, as though urging him forward.

Suddenly, a figure appeared at the edge of the swirling light—a shadowy figure, tall and indistinct. The figure stepped into the light, and Ethan's heart skipped a beat as he recognized the face.

It was King Darius.

His presence was overwhelming. The figure before them was not just a man, but a manifestation of the king's very will—a being that seemed to transcend human form, shrouded in an aura of dark energy. The king's eyes were glowing with a malicious, unnatural light, and his voice was like thunder, deep and resonating, as it boomed through the space.

"Foolish child," King Darius' voice thundered, "Did you really think you could stop me? You cannot control time. You can only delay it, and in the end, I will have what I need."

Ethan's grip tightened on the watch. The power it held was undeniable, but the king's presence seemed to twist the very air around him. The world felt unstable, fragile—like they were standing on the edge of reality itself.

"You think you can stop me by playing with time?" King Darius sneered. "I have mastered it. I have bent it to my will. Your petty watch is nothing more than a toy—an artifact of an age long past."

Ethan's breath caught in his throat. This was the moment of truth—the moment when everything he had learned, everything he had fought for, would come to a head. King Darius, who had spent his life trying to control the flow of time, now stood before him, an embodiment of the very forces Ethan sought to control.

But Ethan wasn't afraid. The watch in his hand seemed to pulse with an almost sentient energy, as though it were alive, guiding him toward something greater. The voice he had heard earlier returned, this time clearer and more urgent.

The key is within you. It is your choice, Ethan. What you decide now will shape the future of all things. Choose wisely.

Ethan's hand shook, not from fear, but from the sheer weight of the decision before him. He could feel the immense power coursing through the watch, through him. It wasn't just a weapon—it was a responsibility, a choice that could change the world.

He looked at King Darius, his expression unwavering. "I won't let you control time," he said, his voice steady, though his heart pounded in his chest. "I won't let you destroy everything."

King Darius' laughter echoed, dark and mocking. "You think you can stop me? You are a child, and this world is mine to command."

But as the king's words faded into the swirling vortex of light, Ethan made his choice. He raised the watch high, the golden surface gleaming in the light, and with a force of will that surprised even him, he pressed the watch's crown.

In an instant, the world around them froze.

Time itself halted.

The swirling vortex around them stopped in its tracks, suspended in a moment of perfect stillness. The forest, the king, and even the very air itself were frozen, caught in the web of time that Ethan had unleashed.

But it wasn't the king who had won—it was Ethan. The power of the watch, combined with his own choices, had created a new path. The king's plans were halted, his hold on time shattered.

For now, the balance had shifted.

BETRAYAL

The moment Ethan had thought he had gained control over time, the watch pulsed once more—stronger, more insistent, as if it were a living, breathing entity. The stillness of the world around them felt like an oppressive weight, an overwhelming silence that left him unsettled. It had worked. For now. But Ethan knew better than to think that the danger was over. Time had stopped, but the future still loomed ahead, uncertain, unstable.

Lila stood beside him, her face pale from the intensity of the moment. Her eyes, once filled with fear, were now laced with awe and wonder at the watch in Ethan's hand.

"You did it," she whispered, barely able to believe what they had just accomplished. "You stopped him... You stopped time."

Ethan glanced down at the watch, its golden surface still glowing faintly in the suspended air. The weight of its power was both empowering and terrifying. The path to the future was open, but now, more than ever, he felt the gravity of their situation. King Darius wasn't one to be defeated so easily. Ethan had only won a brief moment—a temporary pause in the battle for control over time itself. He knew the king would return, and when he did, it would be with even greater power and malice.

"We've only bought ourselves time," Ethan said quietly, his voice tinged with uncertainty. "But time is the most dangerous weapon we have."

Lila nodded, but there was a hesitance in her eyes, a flicker of doubt. She couldn't shake the feeling that something was wrong. The calm they had achieved felt too fragile, too delicate to last. The stillness around them was like a momentary illusion, and Ethan could sense it too.

Suddenly, the sound of approaching footsteps broke the silence, sending a shiver down Ethan's spine. His hand instinctively went to the pocket watch, ready to activate its power once more if necessary. But the footsteps were slow, deliberate. A figure emerged from the shadows of the frozen world—moving freely, untouched by the halt in time.

It was Sebastian.

Sebastian was a trusted ally, one who had been with them since the beginning of their journey. He had been by their side during the worst of their trials, offering guidance and support when things seemed darkest. But as he stepped into the light, his usual calm demeanor was replaced by something else — something that sent a chill through Ethan's bones.

The man's eyes, once warm and compassionate, now gleamed with an eerie coldness. His smile was tight, forced, and there was a subtle, unsettling gleam in his eyes that Ethan had never seen before.

"Sebastian?" Ethan asked, his voice uncertain, the name feeling foreign on his lips. "What are you doing here?"

The man looked at them with an expression that was almost pitying. "You didn't think it would be that easy, did you?" he said softly, his voice laced with an almost amused detachment. "The king's plans are not so easily thwarted. I've been with you from the beginning, Ethan. I know your strengths, your weaknesses, your fears. I know everything about you. You were never meant to win."

Ethan's blood ran cold. The words hung in the air like a heavy fog. "What are you saying? Sebastian, what are you talking about?"

Sebastian stepped closer, his eyes narrowing. "I've been working for King Darius all along, Ethan. You're nothing more than a pawn in a much larger game. A game that's about to come to its final conclusion. You've played your part well, but it's over now. The king is going to win."

Lila took a step back, her hand instinctively reaching for the dagger at her side. "No... No, you can't be serious," she whispered, her voice trembling. "We trusted you."

Sebastian's lips curled into a cruel smile, the last remnants of his former kindness gone. "Trust is a fragile thing, Lila. It was never real. Not between us. Not between any of us. The king has promised me power beyond anything you can imagine. And now, with you two out of the way, he'll get what he's always wanted—control over time itself."

Ethan felt the weight of the betrayal crash down on him like a physical blow. The sense of disbelief was overwhelming. Sebastian, the person he had once trusted with his life, was the very enemy they had been fighting against all this time. The realization hit him hard—there had been no safe haven, no allies they could truly trust. They had been surrounded by shadows from the beginning, each of them hiding their true intentions.

"You don't understand," Ethan said, his voice strained with frustration. "You're not just working for him, you're helping him destroy everything. The king doesn't care about power—he wants to rewrite history. He wants to control time itself. You're not gaining power, Sebastian. You're helping him destroy everything we know."

Sebastian's face remained impassive, his eyes cold and calculating. "You still don't understand, Ethan. This isn't about rewriting history. It's about creating a new world. One where the king is in control of everything—where time is no longer a force of nature, but something to be bent, molded, and shaped to his will. And I will be the one who helps him make it happen."

Ethan felt a rush of anger surge through him. "You're a fool," he spat, his words filled with venom. "You're willing to throw everything away for what? For the king's empty promises? For power that will never truly be yours?"

Sebastian's expression hardened. "You still don't understand. The king is not a man. He is the future. He is the inevitable. And I will stand by him when the world bows before him."

The betrayal stung deeper than any physical wound ever could. Ethan had trusted Sebastian. He had believed that they were on the same side—that they were fighting for the same cause. And now, in the blink of an eye, all of that trust had been shattered.

But there was no time to dwell on the past. The stakes were higher than ever. The king was closer than they realized, and now, with Sebastian as his agent within their ranks, they had to face an even greater threat than before.

Ethan clenched his fists, the watch pulsing with power once more. He would not let Sebastian's treachery be the end of their fight. There was still hope, but it was fading fast.

"You're wrong, Sebastian," Ethan said quietly, his voice steady with determination. "The king may have the power to control time, but he doesn't understand it. Time is not something to be controlled. It's something to be respected. And we will stop him. No matter what."

Sebastian chuckled, his smile cruel and twisted. "You'll see soon enough, Ethan. Time is already on my side. On the king's side."

With that, he turned and vanished into the shadows, leaving Ethan and Lila standing alone in the frozen world, the weight of betrayal heavy in the air.

Ethan and Lila stood in stunned silence, the weight of Sebastian's betrayal settling in like a dark, suffocating fog. The truth was a bitter pill to swallow—one they had never anticipated. Their trusted ally, their friend, had been working for the very king they had been trying to stop. The realization that the person they had relied on was part of the very web of deception they were trying to untangle made the world feel like it was crumbling around them.

Ethan looked down at the pocket watch in his hand, the glimmering timepiece now a reminder of everything they had to lose. Time, once a tool they could manipulate, now felt like an enemy itself—one that was slipping out of their control. The pulse of the watch was faint now, but it carried a heavy, ominous energy. The reality of Sebastian's betrayal was sinking in, and with it came the creeping fear that they were running out of time.

"We need to move," Lila's voice broke through the silence, her words sharp and purposeful. "If Sebastian's working for Darius, then we can't trust anyone—not anymore. We need to get to the heart of his plans. We need to stop him before it's too late."

Ethan nodded, his mind racing as he tried to piece together the new pieces of their situation. Sebastian's betrayal changed everything. They had been blind to the fact that they were never fully safe. In every step of their journey, there had been shadows lurking in the corners, waiting to reveal themselves. And now, Sebastian's true allegiance was out in the open.

"We have to be smart about this," Ethan said, his voice quieter now, the weight of his thoughts pressing on him. "We can't go rushing in without a plan. We need to know where Darius is, what he's doing, and what he's planning next. We can't let him get to the watch. If he controls it, we're done for."

Lila's expression hardened. "We know where he's headed. His plans are in motion—he's already moving toward the Citadel of Time. If he reaches it before we do, the power will shift in his favor. We'll lose everything. And without Sebastian's knowledge of Darius's next moves, we don't have much time to figure out our next steps."

The Citadel of Time. The words echoed in Ethan's mind like a warning. The Citadel was the heart of time itself—the place where the fabric of time could be controlled, manipulated, and rewritten. It was the last place anyone who sought ultimate power over time would want to be. And now, with Sebastian's betrayal, it was a race against time to reach it before the king.

Lila turned away, her expression determined but haunted. "We can't waste time second-guessing ourselves. We know what's at stake. We've lost too much already."

As Ethan and Lila began to move forward, preparing for the next stage of their journey, the once-promising hope they had clung to now felt distant and fragile. Their only allies had been stolen from them, and now it was a fight against not only the king but the very nature of time itself.

They crossed paths with an old merchant who had once offered them help, but even his warm smile felt tinged with suspicion. Time was a currency now, and everyone seemed to have a stake in the game. No one was immune from the chaos that was beginning to unfurl.

As they made their way toward the Citadel, they couldn't shake the feeling that the king was never too far behind. His spies were everywhere, and with Sebastian's knowledge, the search for the pocket watch and its power would escalate quickly. Ethan knew that they were playing a dangerous game. Each step forward was fraught with uncertainty, but turning back was not an option. The king's reach was already too vast, and with every passing moment, the king's influence over time was growing stronger.

But even in the midst of this chaos, there was still something inside of Ethan that refused to give up. He refused to believe that everything they had fought for, everything they had sacrificed, was for nothing. The truth had been revealed, but that didn't mean the end was inevitable.

"We won't let him win," Ethan said, his voice filled with resolve. "No matter what it takes, we'll stop Darius. We'll stop the king from rewriting time itself."

Lila glanced at him, her expression softening, but only for a moment. "And if we don't?" she asked, her voice barely above a whisper.

Ethan turned to face her, his eyes steady and unyielding. "Then we'll make sure that he never has the chance to change history."

The air was thick with the weight of betrayal as Ethan and Lila walked through the darkened forest. The distant echo of the city's unrest still reverberated in the background. Each step felt heavier than the last, as if the very earth beneath them could sense their unease. Ethan clutched the pocket watch tightly in his hand, feeling its pulse beat against his palm like a reminder of everything at stake. It was their only hope now, the key to everything that had been set in motion.

Sebastian's betrayal cut deeper than any physical wound. He was no longer just a friend; he was a traitor, an instrument of Darius's dark agenda. Ethan had always believed in the inherent goodness of people, but now that trust felt like a fragile illusion. He wondered what had truly driven Sebastian to betray them—was it power, fear, or something even darker? And worse, how much damage had Sebastian already caused in his secret dealings with the king?

Lila's voice broke through his thoughts. "Ethan, we need to move faster. The Citadel of Time isn't far now, but Darius is already on our trail. If we don't reach it first, the king will gain control of time, and nothing we've done will matter anymore."

Ethan nodded grimly. He knew that the stakes had never been higher. The Citadel of Time was the very heart of time manipulation, a place that could alter history itself. If Darius reached it before they did, he could rewrite the fabric of time to suit his twisted desires. The power that lay within the Citadel could undo everything they had fought for.

"We're running out of time," Ethan muttered, his voice filled with a sense of urgency that matched the pounding of his heart. "We can't let Darius take control. The watch... it's the key. We need to get to the Citadel, or everything we've done is for nothing."

Lila nodded in agreement, her gaze focused ahead, but Ethan could see the hesitation in her eyes. The betrayal had shattered her as well. She, too, had trusted Sebastian. She had considered him a vital part of their team, and the sting of his betrayal was something she could not simply brush aside. Yet, despite the hurt, Lila remained resolute. There was no time to dwell on the past; their mission was more important than ever.

As they moved through the dense forest, the shadows seemed to close in around them, and the weight of their decision began to sink deeper. There was no way to know who else could be a double agent or who could be watching their every move. Sebastian had been their friend, but now they had to trust no one. The king's spies were likely already tracking them, ready to strike at any moment.

Ethan's thoughts drifted back to the pocket watch. The key to time. But what did that truly mean? The watch held incredible power, a power that no one—especially not Darius—should wield. Ethan knew that they had to protect it at all costs, but the real question was how. Time was a force beyond their comprehension, and now, with the king hunting them, their time was rapidly running out.

"How do we stop him?" Lila asked suddenly, her voice a low whisper, almost as if she were speaking to herself. "How do we stop someone who can control time itself?"

Ethan stopped in his tracks, his mind racing. It was a question that had plagued him since they first encountered the king's plans. Time was a constant force, but to control it was a different matter entirely. Darius's quest for power was not just about ruling over the present—it was about rewriting the past and shaping the future to fit his twisted vision. If Darius succeeded, the world they knew could cease to exist as they understood it. The very laws of nature would bend to his will, and nothing would be beyond his control.

"Maybe the watch isn't just a key," Ethan said slowly, piecing the puzzle together in his mind. "Maybe it's also a lock. We're not supposed to control time, but protect it. If we can reach the Citadel and use the watch properly, we might be able to stop Darius from bending time to his will."

Lila's eyes widened with realization. "So... we don't use it to rewrite history, but to stop him from rewriting it?"

Ethan nodded. "Exactly. The watch could be a tool to block the king's access to the Citadel. If we can activate it at the right moment, we might be able to shut down his access to the Citadel's power. But we need to get there first, and we need to make sure Darius doesn't get his hands on it."

They both knew that it was a long shot, but it was the only plan they had. Time itself seemed to be slipping away from them, and the Citadel of Time loomed ahead as the last remaining bastion of hope. They had to reach it before Darius did, or else everything they had fought for would be lost forever.

Just as they began to move forward, a rustling sound came from behind them. Lila's hand instinctively went to her blade, and Ethan's grip on the pocket watch tightened. They weren't alone.

Out of the darkness emerged a figure—a silhouette cloaked in shadows. Ethan's heart skipped a beat. Could it be another one of Darius's spies? Or perhaps someone else who had been watching them all along? The figure stepped forward, revealing a familiar face, and for a split second, Ethan's breath caught in his throat.

It was Sebastian.

He stood there, his face a mix of regret and determination. In his eyes, there was no longer the glint of deception, but something else—something almost... human. "I never wanted to betray you," he said quietly, his voice strained. "But I had no choice. Darius has a way of getting to people. I was trying to protect you both, but I failed."

Ethan stared at him, unable to speak at first. The emotions inside him were a tangled mess. Betrayal, confusion, anger—but now there was a faint glimmer of something else. Was this the beginning of redemption, or just another trick?

Lila's eyes narrowed, but she remained silent, her hand still resting on the hilt of her blade. "What are you doing here, Sebastian?" she asked, her voice cold but tinged with disbelief. "Why should we trust you now?"

"I don't expect you to trust me," Sebastian said, his voice low and filled with sorrow. "But if we don't stop Darius, we're all doomed. I know the way to the Citadel. Let me help you. I can be the guide you need. But we need to move quickly."

Ethan exchanged a long, hard look with Lila. Trusting Sebastian again was dangerous. But they didn't have many options left.

Finally, Ethan spoke, his voice resolute. "Fine. But if you try anything again, we won't hesitate. We're past the point of second chances."

Sebastian nodded, the weight of his actions apparent in his gaze. "I understand. Let's end this together."

And so, with the looming threat of the king and his power over time, they pressed forward—together, for the first time in what felt like an eternity, and yet, nothing could erase the lingering question: Could they truly stop Darius, or had they already lost?

THE FINAL BATTLE

The silence of the night was heavy, almost suffocating, as Ethan and Lila approached the gates of the Citadel of Time. The massive stone structure loomed before them, its towers reaching high into the sky like ancient guardians of a forgotten age. The air here was thick with power—power that had been dormant for centuries but was now awakening, drawing its strength from the very fabric of time itself. The distant echoes of the king's armies could be heard marching ever closer, their steps like a drumbeat of fate.

With each passing moment, the tension between Ethan and Lila grew. The betrayal of Sebastian, the uncertainty of their own plan, and the overwhelming threat of King Darius's rise to absolute power had turned this journey into something far more than they had ever imagined. This was no longer just a fight to stop a king; this was a battle for the survival of time itself.

Ethan could feel the weight of the pocket watch against his chest, the tiny timepiece that had carried them through their trials and tribulations. It pulsed with an energy that was almost alive, and he could sense that it was more than just a key—it was the last hope of the world. But as they neared the Citadel's entrance, the reality set in. Time was not just a force they could manipulate—it was a force that could break them, too.

Lila turned to him, her face pale under the moonlight, but her eyes were fierce, determined. "This is it, Ethan," she said quietly, her voice unwavering. "No more running. We either stop him now, or everything we've fought for will be lost."

Ethan nodded, swallowing the lump in his throat. His mind raced, recalling everything they had learned along the way—the betrayals, the alliances, the moments of hope that had carried them this far. Yet, there was still one thing they couldn't escape: the king's insatiable hunger for control. Darius had already manipulated so many people, turning them into his puppets. What would happen when he had control over time itself? Ethan shuddered at the thought.

They crossed the threshold into the Citadel, its massive iron doors creaking open, revealing the vast, dimly lit chamber within. The walls seemed to hum with ancient energy, their stones carved with symbols that no one alive could understand. The air inside was colder than any place they had been before, a biting chill that seemed to freeze the very marrow in their bones.

At the far end of the chamber stood a throne, black and imposing, carved from a stone that glimmered faintly, as though it held the power of a thousand lifetimes. And sitting upon that throne, surrounded by swirling dark energy, was King Darius. His eyes glowed with an unnatural light, and the very air around him seemed to warp and shift, as if he were bending the rules of reality itself.

"Ethan," Darius's voice was cold, but there was a cruel amusement in it. "Lila. You're too late. Time is mine now, and nothing you do can change that." His hand lifted, and the room seemed to tremble in response. The walls around them began to pulse with energy, and the very ground beneath their feet seemed to stretch and distort. The Citadel, which had once been a place of balance, now resonated with

Darius's power, a power that threatened to tear the very fabric of existence apart.

Ethan stepped forward, his heart pounding in his chest, but he forced himself to stand tall. He could feel the power of the watch responding, its pulse growing stronger as the distance between them and Darius closed. This was it—the moment they had been preparing for. The battle for the future of time had come, and there was no turning back.

"You don't understand, Darius," Ethan called out, his voice carrying across the vast chamber. "Time isn't something to be controlled. It's meant to be lived, experienced. You're trying to force it into your own image, but you can't—"

Darius's laughter rang out, sharp and echoing through the Citadel. "Oh, Ethan, you still don't understand, do you? Time is not something to be experienced. It's something to be mastered. And now, with this power, I will reshape the world in my image. Everything will be as I see fit."

The king's words twisted through the air, heavy with malice and madness. Ethan could feel the truth of them—Darius was not just after power. He was after total domination, a world where everything bent to his will, where time itself could be erased, rewritten, and twisted. Nothing would be left untouched.

The darkness in the chamber thickened, and a cold wind began to swirl around them. Time itself seemed to be shifting, collapsing, warping. In that moment, Ethan realized what Darius was truly trying to do. The Citadel was not just a place of power—it was a conduit for time itself. Darius had found a way to channel the very essence of time through it, to become its master, to control every moment, every second.

Lila's voice broke through his thoughts, sharp with urgency. "Ethan, the watch! You have to use it! Now!" She was right. This was their only chance. With the king's power threatening to destroy everything, the pocket watch was their last hope.

Ethan pulled the watch from his belt and held it high, feeling its power surge through him. The air around him seemed to crackle with energy, the very fabric of time itself bending in response to the watch's call. He could feel it—a deep, resonant hum that vibrated through his bones. The watch was more than a key;

it was a weapon. A weapon that could stop Darius. But only if he knew how to wield it.

Darius's smile widened as he saw the watch. "Ah, yes. The fabled pocket watch. You think that little trinket will save you? It is nothing more than a relic, a failed attempt to control the flow of time. But you're too late, Ethan. Time is already mine."

With a wave of his hand, Darius summoned a storm of energy, sending a blast of dark power toward them. The very air crackled and hissed with the force of it, and the ground beneath their feet began to shake violently. Ethan barely managed to raise the watch, and in that instant, the timepiece seemed to pulse with light, responding to the king's attack.

A barrier of light erupted from the watch, clashing with Darius's power. The shockwave from the collision sent a tremor through the Citadel, and the ground beneath them cracked. The chamber was filled with the deafening roar of energy colliding—time and space warping, tearing, and shifting in ways that no one could have predicted.

"Impossible!" Darius roared, his eyes widening in disbelief. "No one should be able to stop me!"

Ethan gritted his teeth, his heart racing. This was their chance—the watch wasn't just a tool to control time, it was the key to breaking Darius's grip on it. The barrier of light that surrounded them began to pulse with a blinding intensity, and Ethan could feel the power of time itself channeling through him.

"Together, Lila!" he shouted, his voice filled with determination. Lila stepped forward, her hand resting on her sword's hilt, ready for whatever came next. They had come this far, and there was no turning back.

As the final battle raged, Ethan knew one thing for certain: this was not just a fight for their survival. It was a battle for the very future of time.

The clash of powers—the bright, searing light of Ethan's pocket watch against the swirling darkness of King Darius's wrath—had become the very heartbeat of the Citadel. Each moment stretched out like an eternity as the chamber rocked with the reverberations of their combined forces. The walls groaned under the weight of the battle, and the air crackled with raw energy, bending and warping as though it too were part of the fight.

Darius's eyes glowed brighter with fury, his form shifting and distorting with the force of his rage. The dark tendrils of his power writhed like serpents around him, reaching out toward Ethan and Lila in an attempt to strangle them, to break their resolve. But the light of the pocket watch pushed back, a tangible force in the room, as if time itself were fighting against the king's dominance.

"Do you think you can defeat me with that?" Darius sneered, his voice laced with venom. "You are nothing. Time is mine to command, and I will reshape it as I see fit!"

The ground beneath their feet trembled, the very foundation of the Citadel threatening to collapse under the pressure of their battle. Ethan gritted his teeth, his grip tightening on the watch. He could feel its power—its ancient magic—coursing through him, filling him with an energy he had never known before. But it wasn't enough. Not yet.

Lila, ever steadfast by his side, watched him closely, her eyes sharp with focus. "Ethan, you have to synchronize the watch with the flow of time itself.

Use its connection to the past and the future. It's the only way we can stop him."

Her words pierced through the chaos of the moment like a beacon of clarity. The key to defeating Darius was not just using the watch as a weapon—it was understanding its true nature. The pocket watch was not simply a tool of control, but a bridge between all points in time. If they could harness that, they could sever Darius's hold on the Citadel—and on time itself.

Ethan's heart raced as he concentrated on the watch, focusing on the steady, rhythmic pulse of its energy. He closed his eyes and reached deep within himself, tapping into the ancient knowledge he had uncovered during their journey—the teachings of the Watchmakers, the whispers of the Time Keepers. He could feel it now: the watch was alive, not just a mere object but a living conduit to the flow of time. It was the key to everything. He only had to unlock its potential.

The light of the watch blazed brighter, and the surrounding darkness seemed to recoil from it, as if Darius's power could no longer hold its ground against the force of time itself. The swirling tendrils of darkness began to dissipate, fading into the ether as the watch's glow intensified.

Darius's laughter faltered, his confident smirk beginning to slip. "No… this can't be…" he hissed, his voice thick with disbelief. The dark energy around him flared in a desperate attempt to reassert its dominance, but Ethan felt the shift in the air—the balance was changing. Time, in its infinite complexity, was beginning to turn against Darius.

The Citadel itself seemed to respond. The ancient stones beneath their feet trembled as the very essence of time surged through them, cascading in waves of energy. The walls cracked, the intricate carvings of forgotten eras shimmering with new life. Ethan could feel the echoes of the past and future all around him, a pulse that resonated deep within his soul. This was the true power of the pocket watch—it wasn't just a key to control time, but a force that could reshape the very fabric of reality.

Lila stepped forward, her sword raised in preparation for what was to come. "We can do this,

Ethan. Together," she said, her voice steady even in the face of overwhelming darkness.

With a final, determined breath, Ethan opened his eyes and focused the energy of the watch into a single, concentrated beam. The power surged outward, cutting through the air like a knife. The blast of light collided with the dark tendrils, unraveling them in an instant. Darius screamed in frustration as the very fabric of his power unraveled before him, his grip on the Citadel weakening with every passing second.

"No!" Darius roared, his form shifting wildly as the watch's power continued to pierce through his defenses. "You can't—!"

But it was too late.

In that moment, the Citadel seemed to crack open. A surge of blinding light erupted from the heart of the chamber, engulfing Darius in a whirlwind of time itself. The king's scream echoed as the very essence of his being was pulled into the vortex, his power being ripped away, his control over time vanishing like sand through the fingers of a dying storm.

Ethan and Lila shielded their eyes from the blinding light, feeling the overwhelming pull of time as it twisted and reformed around them. The Citadel began to collapse, its walls crumbling as the king's influence faded away. The air was thick with the energy of time, and the space around them seemed to bend and stretch as though reality itself were being rewritten.

As the light began to dim, and the rumbling of the collapsing Citadel slowed, Ethan and Lila stood in the center of the now-ruined chamber, breathing heavily. The storm of energy had passed, and for the first time in what felt like an eternity, there was silence.

Darius was gone.

The pocket watch, still in Ethan's hand, had returned to its steady pulse, no longer emanating the overwhelming surge of power that had once threatened to tear the world apart. It was as if the watch had found its place once more—no longer a weapon, but a guide. A guide to balance, to harmony, to the endless flow of time.

But the battle was not over.

The Citadel had fallen, but the world outside still lay in ruins. The scars of the past would not heal overnight, and there were still challenges ahead. But for the first time, Ethan and Lila knew that they had succeeded in their mission: Time, in all its complexity, was free once more. And the future, for the first time in a long while, was full of possibility.

The crumbling Citadel, once a symbol of King Darius's overwhelming power, now lay in ruins, its jagged walls scattered in the wake of their final confrontation. The smoke of the destruction hung thick in the air, as if the world itself had exhaled a heavy sigh, relieved to be free from the king's tyranny. Yet, the battle, in all its intensity, had left its mark—on the Citadel, on the land, and on Ethan and Lila.

Ethan stood still for a moment, his breath shallow and ragged. His hand still clutched the pocket watch, the once-glowing object now dimmed, its power no longer pulsing with the same intensity. The weight of what had just transpired began to sink in—the king, the twisted ruler who had sought to control time itself, was gone. The ancient evil that had plagued their world was no more. But the silence that followed the chaos was not peaceful. It was pregnant with uncertainty, a heavy quiet that weighed on their hearts.

Lila, still standing beside him, was the first to speak. Her voice was soft, but resolute. "It's over, Ethan. We did it."

Ethan looked over at her, his eyes filled with a mix of exhaustion and disbelief. It was hard to comprehend that after everything they had been through—after the endless dangers, the sacrifices, and the unimaginable battles—this was the end of it. Or, at least, the end of this particular struggle.

But even as they stood in the shattered remnants of the Citadel, they knew the war for the future was far from over. King Darius had not only sought to control time but had corrupted it, tearing the fabric of history and the future itself. The damage he had done was vast, and though they had defeated him, the consequences of his actions would ripple through time, changing things in ways they could not yet understand.

Ethan turned his attention back to the pocket watch in his hand. Its surface, once tarnished and cracked, now seemed to radiate a calm, steady light. The power was still there, but it had changed—become more serene, more controlled. Time itself, it seemed, had found its balance again.

Lila stepped closer, her gaze fixed on the watch. "What now?" she asked, her voice tinged with both hope and apprehension.

Ethan met her eyes, the weight of his decision heavy on his shoulders. He knew the answer, but it was hard to put into words, especially after everything they had just witnessed. The Citadel was destroyed, and King Darius was no more, but the world outside still lay in turmoil. The scars left by the tyrant's reign would take time to heal, and the damage he had done to time itself would need to be repaired.

He held the watch up, his fingers trembling slightly. "Now, we fix what he broke."

A surge of power radiated from the watch, a wave of energy that pulsed out into the world, sweeping over the land like a breath of fresh air. Time itself seemed to ripple, as though the very fabric of reality was reweaving itself—somehow, in some way, beginning to heal from the wounds Darius had inflicted. It was not instantaneous, not perfect, but it was a start.

Lila watched in awe as the energies of the watch radiated outward, the ruins of the Citadel seeming to shimmer with a new vitality. The destruction that had once threatened to consume everything was beginning to reverse. The broken walls seemed to knit themselves together, the dark energy that had pervaded the place slowly dissipating. It was as though time itself was being given the opportunity to restore what had been lost.

Ethan took a deep breath, feeling a strange sense of peace wash over him. He could sense the changes in the world—the slow, almost imperceptible return of balance. The watch was not just a tool of destruction; it was a tool of restoration, of healing. It was as though it had chosen him, or perhaps he had chosen it, to be the protector of time. But what did that mean? What responsibility lay ahead?

"The future is ours to shape," Ethan murmured, more to himself than to Lila. He turned to her, his eyes filled with a renewed sense of purpose. "But we can't do it alone."

Lila nodded, her expression serious. "No. We never could." She paused, her gaze sweeping over the desolate landscape. "But we've learned that together, we can rebuild. We can mend what was broken."

As the last remnants of King Darius's dark influence faded into the ether, Ethan and Lila exchanged a look—a silent understanding passing between them. They had come so far, faced so many impossible odds. And while the world was still scarred from the tyrant's reign, there was hope. There was a future.

The pocket watch, now calm and steady in Ethan's grasp, held the potential to rewrite time—but only if they used it wisely. The temptation to control, to manipulate, would always be there, but they had learned something crucial throughout their journey: power without wisdom was as dangerous as the tyrant they had just defeated.

Lila gave a soft smile, the first real one in what felt like ages. "Let's make sure we don't lose sight of what matters."

Ethan returned her smile, his heart lighter than it had been in a long time. Together, they had found the strength to defeat a god-like tyrant, to challenge the very fabric of reality. And together, they would shape a future where time flowed freely, without the tyranny of one man.

"Let's rebuild," Ethan said quietly, his voice resolute. "And let's make sure it never happens again."

They turned away from the crumbled Citadel, the watch still glowing softly in Ethan's hand. There was no more need for haste, no more urgency. The battle was won. But their journey—though its fiercest challenges had passed—was only just beginning.

RESTORING BALANCE

The world had been fractured, torn apart by the chaos of King Darius's reign. Time itself had been twisted, bent to the whims of a man who sought dominion over everything—over the past, the present, and the future. The ancient magic of the pocket watch, now fully awakened, pulsed softly in Ethan's grasp. It was both an instrument of immense power and a burden—one that weighed heavily on his shoulders. This small object, once a mere curiosity, now held the responsibility of restoring what had been broken.

The sky above them was an uneven patchwork of colors, as if the heavens themselves were still healing. Ethan stared at the horizon, where the land seemed to shift and pulse with energy. The destruction left by Darius had not been limited to the Citadel. The very fabric of time had been damaged, leaving rifts in history, fractures in the natural order. The rivers no longer flowed in their usual paths, the seasons seemed out of sync, and the winds carried whispers of forgotten events—echoes of what could have been.

Lila stood beside him, her eyes tracing the faint lines of energy that still rippled across the earth. She was silent, sensing the enormity of what they had to do. Ethan could feel the pulse of the watch in his hand, its vibrations synchronizing with his heartbeat. It was as though the watch was not just a tool, but an extension of himself—its magic now part of him, part of their journey.

"We can't fix everything, can we?" Lila's voice broke the silence, her gaze turning to him with an unreadable expression.

Ethan shook his head, his grip on the watch tightening. "No, we can't. Some things are too far gone. But we can restore balance. We can make sure that what Darius did... doesn't last. We can make sure that the future remains ours to shape."

It was not a promise of perfection, but it was the best they could do. And in a world where time itself had been bent and twisted, restoring balance was no small feat. Ethan knew that he wasn't just trying to fix the physical world around him; he was trying to fix time itself. The weight of that task felt immense, almost unbearable.

The pocket watch seemed to sense his thoughts, its energy amplifying in response to his determination. The gears inside it whirred, the glass face shining with an ethereal light, as if beckoning him forward. Ethan knew that the moment had come. He had to act, to make the choice that would either restore the natural flow of time or risk destroying everything further. The consequences of this decision would echo across the ages, and the weight of that knowledge pressed down on him.

He glanced at Lila. She had always been the voice of reason, the one who reminded him of the bigger picture when he was too focused on the immediate dangers. And now, even in this moment of finality, she gave him a silent nod—a reassurance, a confirmation that they were in this together. He wasn't alone. Not now. Not ever.

Ethan closed his eyes and took a deep breath, feeling the energy of the watch flow into him, filling the empty spaces inside him where uncertainty once lingered. The time had come to act, and he knew he couldn't wait any longer. With a swift motion, he raised the watch high, letting the light from its face fill the sky. The world seemed to hold its breath, as though it too understood the gravity of the moment.

Suddenly, the air around them crackled with energy. The vibrations from the watch spread like ripples across a pond, expanding outward with a force that seemed to reach into every corner of the earth, touching the past, the present, and the future. Ethan felt the pulse of time itself—the heartbeat of the universe. Every tick of the watch, every turn of its gears, resonated through him, weaving the threads of history back into place. The fractures began to mend, slowly but surely, as the watch's power worked its magic.

It was a delicate balance, a fine thread that had to be pulled tight, but not too tight. Too much force, and time could collapse in on itself. Too little, and the damage Darius had caused would remain, festering and growing until it consumed everything. Ethan focused all his energy, channeling the watch's magic with precision. He could feel the watch's power responding to his will, aligning with his intentions, guiding him as though it understood the responsibility of what was at stake.

The world around them began to shift. The landscape, once warped by the tyrant's manipulation, slowly returned to its natural state. The trees, which had once withered in the unnatural climate created by Darius's reign, began to bloom again. Rivers started to flow once more, their currents regaining their familiar paths. The winds, once caught in a strange, timeless stasis, began to blow again, carrying with them the scents of fresh earth and the promise of new beginnings.

And yet, even as the physical world began to heal, there was more to the task at hand. Ethan could feel the deeper currents of time, the places where the past had been altered, the places where memories had been lost. History was not a single straight line but a complex web of interconnected events, and Darius had tried to sever some of those threads entirely. The damage was not just in what had been destroyed, but in what had been erased.

Ethan focused on these moments, reaching into the fabric of time itself, pulling at the loose threads, carefully weaving them back into place. He could see flashes of the past—people, places, moments that had once been lost to the twisted manipulation of time. He felt their essence, their memories, their experiences, as they flickered back into existence. It was not an easy task. Time was a fragile thing, and the consequences of altering it were far-reaching. But with the power of the watch, he could feel it—slowly, painfully, but surely—beginning to heal.

Lila watched him with an intensity that matched his own. She could see the strain in his expression, the way his hands trembled slightly as they held the watch. She could feel the weight of his focus, the way he was both becoming part of the watch's power and yet maintaining control over it. It was a delicate balance, one that only he could achieve.

The landscape around them shifted again, this time more subtly. The world was beginning to heal—slowly, surely—but the work was not yet complete. Ethan's heart raced, the ticking of the watch echoing in his ears. The future was in motion, and the watch's magic was no longer just a tool for restoration; it had become a conduit, a bridge between the fractured past and an uncertain future.

Ethan could feel the fabric of reality bending and shifting around him, as though the universe itself was testing his resolve. The pulse of the pocket watch was growing stronger, reverberating through the air like the hum of a distant thunderstorm. It was a power that had once been locked away, but now, it was alive and pulsing with life, desperate to fulfill its purpose. Ethan's mind raced with the knowledge that he was not simply undoing the harm Darius had caused; he was restoring time to its rightful course, a task more daunting than any challenge he had ever faced.

Every tick of the watch echoed like the turning of a page in a book that had been lost to the ages. The past was not just a series of events; it was a living entity, filled with stories, moments, and decisions that shaped the world. And now, these moments were bleeding back into existence, filling the world with their resonance. Faces long forgotten reappeared, their lives once again interwoven into the grand tapestry of history. Yet, for every victory, there was a lingering unease in Ethan's heart. How could one person truly restore the flow of time? What would be the consequences of his actions?

Lila's voice, low and steady, broke his concentration, bringing him back to the present. "Are you sure this is the right way, Ethan?" she asked, her eyes filled with concern but also a spark of hope. "Can you really mend what was broken?"

Ethan did not reply immediately. Instead, he closed his eyes, letting the power of the watch wash over him. The magic was unlike anything he had ever felt before. It was ancient, boundless, and yet terrifying in its capacity to reshape the world. It was not a magic to be wielded lightly, and he could feel the immense weight of responsibility that came with it. Still, deep within him, he knew that this was the only way to prevent the future from becoming as fractured as the past had been.

"I don't know," he finally admitted, his voice soft but resolute. "But it's the only choice we have. We can't let Darius's manipulation of time stand. If we don't act now, there may not be a future left to save."

With a final, steadying breath, Ethan focused on the watch once more, allowing its light to engulf him. The world around them seemed to blur, as though the air itself was thick with energy. He could see flashes of the past—the moments where history had been twisted. The ancient kingdoms, once vibrant with life, now lay dormant in their broken states, frozen in time by Darius's cruel magic. The lives of countless people, their hopes and dreams, their joys and sorrows, had been cast aside like forgotten stories, their threads pulled out of the great loom of time.

The watch vibrated with intensity, as if recognizing the delicate nature of what was being attempted. Ethan felt the magic surge through him, coursing down his arm and into the core of the earth beneath his feet. He wasn't just fixing the world; he was realigning it with the natural flow of time. He could see events unfolding, streams of history cascading through his mind like a river, and with each turn of the watch's gears, those events began to find their proper places once again. It was a painstaking process, one that required not just strength but precision. Every decision, every moment, rippled outwards, affecting everything around him.

Lila watched, helpless yet supportive, as Ethan battled with the forces of time itself. The magic emanating from the watch had become a swirling vortex, its power too immense to be fully understood. It was almost as if Ethan himself had become part of the fabric of time, a conduit for its repair. But with each passing moment, the danger of overextending himself grew. Time was not a thing that could be bent indefinitely. There had to be a limit.

"I can feel it," Ethan muttered, his brow furrowed in concentration. "The imbalance... it's like a knot in time. I have to undo it... but it's so much bigger than I thought."

Lila stepped closer, placing a hand on his shoulder. "Take it slow. We don't need to fix everything all at once. You're trying to heal the world, but it's not all going to happen in an instant. You can't carry the weight of all that history."

Ethan nodded, though he wasn't sure if he believed her words. How could he slow down when the very fabric of existence was unraveling before his eyes? But as he focused on the power of the watch, he felt something new—a sense of connection, not just to time itself but to the people whose lives were intricately woven into it. It was as though the watch wasn't simply repairing history; it was reuniting him with the souls of those who had been affected by

Darius's tyranny. He could feel their hopes, their fears, their dreams, and for a moment, it seemed as though they were with him, urging him on.

It was then that he realized something: this wasn't just about fixing what had been broken. It was about remembering. It was about honoring the lives that had been lost, the moments that had been erased. It was about giving those stories their place in the world again.

The watch's light flickered and pulsed, growing brighter as the cracks in time began to heal. Ethan, with renewed strength, focused on the key moments—those moments that were most fragile, the ones that had been at the heart of Darius's manipulation. He could feel the energy shifting, the past being woven back into the present. The world was beginning to right itself.

But there was still more to be done.

Ethan glanced at Lila, his face weary but determined. "We're not done yet, Lila. There's still more. We need to make sure the future is secure too."

Lila gave him a small, reassuring smile. "Then let's make sure we don't repeat the past. We've seen what happens when we let power go unchecked. This time, we'll do things differently."

With the weight of the world shifting in their hands, Ethan and Lila turned toward the future, knowing that the journey was far from over. The restoration of balance was just the beginning. They had to make sure that time, once again, flowed freely, without the shadow of Darius's tyranny hanging over it.

And though the road ahead was uncertain, one thing was clear: they would face whatever came next together.

The swirling vortex of light from the pocket watch intensified. Each passing second felt like an eternity, and the atmosphere around Ethan was heavy with the weight of the task he was performing. The energy emanating from the watch was both overwhelming and awe-inspiring. As Ethan focused, his hands trembling, the intricacies of the moment unfolded before his mind's eye.

The universe seemed to listen to his every thought, every flicker of his resolve, as he sought to mend the fractured timelines. The watch had become an extension of himself—its power intertwined with his spirit, as if it were drawing on his very essence. Each turn of the gears felt like a step deeper into the cosmic rhythm of existence itself. The forces of time, vast and incomprehensible, were flowing through him, yet Ethan was determined not to falter.

He could feel the very essence of time wrapping itself around him, each second like a living pulse, each moment a thread weaving into the grand tapestry of existence. It was both humbling and terrifying. The weight of the past, present, and future rested on his shoulders, and yet, within that weight, he felt a strange sense of purpose. He was not just restoring what had been broken; he was part of something far larger than he had ever imagined—an eternal force that had always been in motion, a force he had now learned to navigate.

Despite the progress Ethan was making, something lingered at the back of his mind. The power of the watch was immense, yes, but its true cost was becoming clearer by the minute. As time bent and snapped back into place, a deep fatigue began to take root in him. He felt as if he were pulling on strings that were far too delicate to handle, forcing events back into order like a surgeon stitching together a wound that threatened to tear open again.

"Ethan, you need to be careful," Lila's voice broke through his reverie, a gentle yet firm reminder. She could sense the toll it was taking on him, the way his eyes seemed to glaze over with the sheer weight of the watch's magic. She had seen him in battle, in danger, but this was different. This was a battle against time itself, and it wasn't just his body that was at risk—his very soul seemed to be intertwined with the task at hand.

He nodded slowly, his eyes still fixed on the shimmering portal of energy the watch had created. "I'm fine," he murmured, though his voice betrayed him. His strength was waning, and he could feel the strain of the task bearing down on him. The light from the watch flickered as though even it could sense his weakening resolve. The magic was not infinite. He had been pushing it to its limits, and the lines between him and the watch were beginning to blur.

"I have to finish this, Lila. It's the only way." His voice was low but resolute, as though he was trying to convince himself more than her. He had no other choice. There could be no turning back.

Lila stepped closer, placing a reassuring hand on his shoulder. "We'll face it together, Ethan. You don't have to carry this alone."

Ethan closed his eyes for a moment, his thoughts settling into a quiet calm. She was right. He had always been a solitary figure, burdened by the weight of his destiny. But now, in this moment, he realized that the future could not be shaped by one person alone. It had never been about him—it was about all of them. Every person, every moment, every choice made had led to this point.

"I know," Ethan whispered, opening his eyes to meet hers. "But it has to be me who makes this final choice."

With a deep, steadying breath, he refocused on the task at hand. The watch pulsed with renewed energy as he reached the final step in the restoration process. The cracks in time that had once seemed insurmountable now felt more like cracks in a fragile shell, ready to be mended.

He took hold of the watch, feeling its weight, and turned its gears once more. This time, however, the light was different. It was not just the light of restoration—it was the light of rebirth, of creation itself. A surge of energy coursed through his veins, and for a brief, fleeting moment, Ethan felt as if he were standing at the very edge of time, gazing into the infinite expanse of possibility.

With one final turn, the universe held its breath. The fractured timeline, once torn asunder, began to heal. The world began to right itself, the threads of history once again woven into their proper places. The darkness that had spread across the land, the distortion caused by Darius's manipulation of time, began to fade. The kingdom was no longer fractured. The people, the places, and the events that had been lost, now found their rightful place in the continuum of time.

But it wasn't just the world that changed. Ethan, too, felt something deep within himself shift. He wasn't the same person who had first picked up the watch.

He was different now—more connected to the world, to time itself, and to the people he had fought so hard to protect. The sense of power he had felt when he first held the watch was now tempered with a deep understanding of its consequences. Time was not a force to be manipulated without care; it was a delicate, fragile thing that required respect.

The watch's glow began to dim, its power spent, its magic now returning to the realm from which it had come. Ethan slowly lowered it, feeling the weight of its responsibility lift from his hands. It was done. The world had been restored, the timeline set back on course, and the threat of Darius was no more.

But even as the watch's power receded, a part of Ethan's soul remained tethered to the knowledge that balance, while restored, was fragile. The universe was no longer in immediate danger, but time itself would always remain a force to be reckoned with. He could not undo the past entirely, and he could not predict what the future would bring. But for now, the present was secure, and that was enough.

Ethan looked to Lila, her face full of hope and relief. They had done it. Together, they had faced the impossible and come out victorious. The journey had been long, and the cost had been great, but in the end, they had saved the world.

As the last of the magical light faded, they stood in silence, the weight of their accomplishment settling around them. They had not only restored balance to the world, but they had also restored something in themselves—the understanding that they could face whatever came next, together.

And with that, they knew their journey was far from over. It was only the beginning.

BACK TO THE PRESENT

Ethan stood in the heart of the ancient forest, the place where it had all began. The final moments of their battle had brought him here—back to this very spot, to the reality he had once known. The world he had returned to seemed so ordinary now, its simplicity almost overwhelming after everything he had seen and experienced. The wind blew gently through the trees, rustling the leaves in a soothing, familiar rhythm. The birds sang their melodies, and the air felt crisp with the hint of autumn. It was as if nothing had changed, as though the journey, the struggles, and the victories had been nothing more than a fleeting dream.

Yet, Ethan knew better. He could feel it in the depths of his being. Everything had changed. He had changed.

The pocket watch, now dull and lifeless, was still clasped tightly in his hand. Its magic had faded, its power spent, yet the weight of its existence in his life would linger forever. It had been a symbol of both his greatest strength and his greatest challenge—a reminder of the burden he had borne, the immense responsibility he had carried to restore balance to time itself. He could not simply discard it, even if it no longer hummed with the energy it once did.

He glanced around the familiar landscape, but it felt different, almost foreign. The world had been so vivid and full of wonder during his adventure—every step felt like it had ripples of significance, each action a catalyst for a greater purpose. But here, now, in the present, everything was just... ordinary. The smell of the earth beneath his feet, the rustle of the leaves, the distant hum of a brook—these were things he had once taken for granted. Now, they felt both comforting and somehow hollow. He had seen too much. He had experienced too much to go back to a life that now seemed insignificant in comparison.

Lila stood beside him, her presence a grounding force. She, too, seemed to be struggling with the transition. The weight of their shared journey was still heavy in the air between them. But as she looked at him, her eyes softened, filled with understanding. She had, too, been changed by everything they had endured.

"We made it," she said softly, her voice still tinged with the awe of what they had accomplished. "We really made it."

Ethan nodded, his heart heavy with the knowledge that their journey was truly over. At least in this time. They had fought for the future, for the balance of time itself, and now that battle was won. But how could they return to their lives, knowing what they had seen? How could they live with the knowledge that they had shaped the course of history, altered the very fabric of existence?

He could feel the weight of that question pressing down on him. The adventure, the hardships, the sacrifices—all of it had led to this moment. But the aftermath was something he had not fully prepared for. His life would never be the same. How could it be?

"Do you ever wonder if things will go back to the way they were?" Ethan asked, his voice barely a whisper, as if speaking too loudly would make the world around him shatter. "If we're really back to where we started? Or if something—everything—is different now?"

Lila turned to face him, her eyes filled with the quiet wisdom that had developed in her over the course of their travels. She had always been the one to ground him, to remind him of the bigger picture. "Maybe things will never be the same," she said thoughtfully. "But maybe that's not such a bad thing. Maybe we're not supposed to go back to the way things were. Maybe we're meant to carry forward what we've learned, to let it shape us into who we need to be now."

Ethan let her words settle in his mind. She was right, in a way. There was no going back. They couldn't undo what had been done. The past was sealed, the future uncertain. But in this present moment, they had the opportunity to move forward—not just as individuals, but as individuals who had seen and understood the power of time itself.

As he stood there, his hand still clutching the watch, a wave of emotion washed over him. The adventure had been hard, grueling even, but it had also been full of wonder and discovery. The things he had seen, the people he had met, the sacrifices he had made—all of it had changed him in ways he could never fully articulate.

"I'm different now," Ethan whispered to himself. He wasn't sure if it was a statement of grief or relief, but it was the truth. He was different. The innocence of his former life, the simplicity of his small village existence, was gone. It had been replaced by something more complex, something more profound. The weight of what they had accomplished, the knowledge that they had not only fought for themselves but for the very fabric of existence, settled into him like a second skin.

But even as the weight of it all pressed down on him, there was something else stirring within him—a sense of hope. The kind of hope that was forged through struggle, through overcoming insurmountable odds. The kind of hope that lived in the hearts of those who had fought not just for themselves, but for others. The kind of hope that could endure, no matter how bleak the world seemed.

Ethan looked up at Lila, his heart lifting just a little. "We've changed the world, Lila. And now, we have to live in it."

Lila smiled softly, her gaze unwavering. "And we will. Together. Whatever comes next, we'll face it. We always will."

They stood in silence for a moment, the weight of their shared journey heavy between them. And as the sun began to set, casting a warm golden light across the landscape, Ethan felt a quiet peace begin to settle in his heart. It wasn't the peace of resolution, for there would always be more battles to fight, more struggles to overcome. But it was the peace of knowing that, whatever came next, they were ready for it.

The world around them had changed, but so had they. And that, Ethan knew, was all that mattered.

As the last remnants of twilight painted the sky in soft hues of purple and orange, Ethan and Lila stood at the edge of the ancient forest, the dense trees now silhouetted against the fading light. The weight of their past adventure still hung between them, palpable like the scent of rain before a storm. Though the landscape around them appeared unchanged, it felt distant, as though the world they had once known was no longer entirely their own.

Ethan turned his gaze towards the pocket watch, still nestled in his hand. The metal was cold against his skin, its surface marred by the passage of time—both literal and figurative. It had been the key to their journey, the tool that had carried them through countless battles, struggles, and moments of despair. Its power had been immense, yet now, it was a hollow relic of a life that was no longer his. The watch, once filled with light and energy, had returned to its former state, a simple object of timekeeping. But to Ethan, it was so much more. It was a reminder of the past he had lived, the people he had met, and the incredible journey he had undertaken. And despite its diminishing power, it was a part of him now, a part of the history he had shaped with his own hands.

"I keep wondering," Ethan spoke slowly, his voice tinged with the weight of his thoughts, "if the world is truly the same. If all the things we did, all the moments we faced… if they've really left their mark. I feel like something's shifted, like things should be different. But how can they be? We've returned to the same place, the same time. The events of the past feel like they happened to someone else."

Lila's eyes softened as she listened to him. She understood. She, too, had felt that disorienting sense of disconnect when they had first returned. Their journey had spanned not just space, but time itself. They had fought in ancient lands, navigated through turbulent futures, and encountered realities that defied comprehension. And now, back in the present, it felt almost surreal, as though they were out of sync with the world around them.

She placed a hand on Ethan's shoulder, grounding him in the present. "Maybe it's not about the world being the same," she said quietly. "Maybe it's about us being the ones who've changed. We've carried something back with us—a deeper understanding, a new sense of purpose. The world around us might not have changed, but we have. And that's what matters."

Ethan turned to look at her, her words resonating deeply within him. He had always known that their adventure would alter them in ways they couldn't fully comprehend. But hearing it articulated out loud brought the weight of those changes into sharper focus. They had faced unimaginable challenges, fought alongside allies who had been as real as the ground beneath their feet, and lost parts of themselves in the process. And yet, they had survived. They had prevailed. But the person Ethan was now, the version of himself that stood here in the quiet forest, was not the same person who had first discovered the pocket watch. He was irrevocably changed, shaped by every experience, every choice, and every sacrifice.

He looked around at the familiar landscape, now bathed in the golden light of the setting sun. It was the same world, the same forest they had left behind. But to Ethan, it was different now. He had learned that even the smallest actions could ripple across time, affecting not only the present but the future as well. He had learned that nothing was truly permanent, that time was fluid and ever-shifting, and that the balance of the world rested not in grand gestures, but in the quiet choices made in the heart of every individual.

A soft breeze stirred the leaves of the trees, and Ethan could hear the distant sound of the river that had once felt so distant, so untouchable. Now, it felt close, like an old friend, a companion that had been with him throughout his journey. The world, though unchanged on the surface, seemed to welcome him back, as if acknowledging the transformation he had undergone.

But there was still a lingering question at the back of his mind—what now? They had saved the world. They had restored the balance. But what did the future hold for them now? Could they return to their lives as they once were? Or was this the beginning of a new journey altogether?

Lila seemed to read his thoughts, her gaze turning towards the horizon. "You're wondering what comes next, aren't you?" she asked softly.

Ethan nodded. "I don't know. I feel like there's still so much to do. So many questions left unanswered."

Lila smiled, her eyes sparkling with a sense of quiet certainty. "That's because there always will be. Time doesn't stop just because we've changed it. It keeps moving, and so must we. But maybe... maybe that's the beauty of it. The journey never truly ends, Ethan. We might be back in the present, but we're forever changed by what we've experienced. And maybe that's enough. Maybe the real journey is learning how to carry what we've learned and let it shape the lives we choose to lead."

Ethan took a deep breath, feeling the weight of her words settle within him. She was right. The journey might have brought them back to the same place, but it had also opened up an entirely new chapter of their lives. They had grown. They had learned. They had seen the world in ways most could never imagine. And now, it was time to carry that wisdom forward, to live in the world they had saved, but to do so as different people—people who understood the true value of time, and the fragility of existence.

As the last rays of the sun dipped below the horizon, casting a soft glow over the world around them, Ethan made a silent promise to himself. He would not waste the gift he had been given. He would live fully, knowing that time was a precious and fleeting thing. And, above all, he would honor the lessons learned during his incredible journey—lessons that would guide him for the rest of his life.

He turned to Lila, a renewed sense of purpose settling in his chest. "You're right. We're not the same. But that's okay. We've earned the right to move forward."

Lila smiled, her hand resting gently in his. "And whatever comes next, we'll face it together. Because the journey isn't just about what we've done—it's about how we continue to grow."

And with that, they began their walk back toward the village, the home that had once felt so distant, but now felt like the beginning of something new. Something better.

The quiet hum of the world filled the air as Ethan and Lila walked side by side, their footsteps light on the soft earth beneath them. The journey back to the village was one of reflection—each step carrying with it the weight of the past, the lessons learned, and the realization that time itself had shaped them in ways they had never anticipated. The village, nestled in the valley, was coming into view, its buildings peaceful against the backdrop of the setting sun. The winding river, now familiar and comforting, sparkled like a ribbon of light cutting through the landscape.

As they neared the village, Ethan couldn't help but feel a sense of disbelief. Everything was so normal, so ordinary. The children were playing in the streets, the village merchants haggled over produce, and the farmers tended to their livestock with familiar routines. It was the same life they had left behind — yet, to Ethan, it felt entirely different. His mind could scarcely reconcile the peacefulness of this moment with the storm of memories that churned inside him. He had fought battles across centuries, walked through time as though it were a living thing, and yet, here he was, returning to the simplicity of the present.

"Do you think the people here will ever understand what happened?" Ethan asked, his voice barely above a whisper. "Will they ever know what we did to save them?"

Lila glanced at him, a soft smile tugging at the corner of her lips. "They might never know the specifics," she said, her tone thoughtful. "But what's important is that we know. We made a difference, even if it's not obvious to anyone else. Sometimes, the smallest acts of courage are the ones that leave the deepest marks on the world."

Ethan nodded, letting her words sink into his heart. It was true. The world didn't need to remember the exact moments of their adventure, the battles they had fought, or the powers they had wielded. What mattered was that they had changed the course of time itself, had altered the future for the better. In the grand scheme of things, that was all that mattered. Their efforts, their struggles, and their sacrifices would be woven into the fabric of the world—unseen but eternal.

As they walked into the heart of the village, Ethan felt an overwhelming sense of gratitude for the life he had once known. He thought of his family, his friends, and the simple joys of everyday life. The quiet mornings, the laughter shared around the dinner table, the comfort of a familiar place. All of it had seemed so insignificant before his journey, but now, it felt precious. Fragile. He knew now that time could slip away in an instant, that nothing was permanent, and that every moment was a gift. He would never take it for granted again.

They reached the village square, where the townspeople had gathered for the evening celebration. The air was thick with the sounds of music and laughter, and the scent of freshly baked bread and roasting meats wafted through the air. It was a scene of normalcy, of peace—a peace they had fought for, and one that they now had the privilege to enjoy.

Ethan turned to Lila, his eyes full of gratitude. "I don't know how to thank you," he said softly. "You've been with me every step of the way, through the darkest moments and the brightest victories."

Lila's gaze softened, and she placed a hand gently on his arm. "We were in this together, Ethan. We always were. There's no need for thanks. We made this journey as equals, as friends."

Ethan smiled, the weight of the world no longer heavy on his shoulders. He realized, in that moment, that the true power of their adventure lay not in the grand victories or the incredible feats they had accomplished. It was in the relationships they had forged, the bonds they had strengthened, and the trust they had placed in one another. It was in the love and the understanding that had blossomed between them, and the knowledge that they would always carry a piece of each other with them, no matter where life took them.

As the sun dipped below the horizon, casting a golden glow over the village, Ethan turned to look at the pocket watch one last time. It was still in his hand, though its power had long since faded. He could feel its weight, not as an object of immense power, but as a symbol of everything he had learned. Time, like the watch, could be fleeting. It could be fragile, unpredictable, and often beyond control. But it was also a gift. A gift to be cherished, to be spent wisely, and to be shared with those who mattered most.

With a final glance at the watch, Ethan tucked it safely into his pocket. The future was uncertain, but the present was something to be savored, something to be embraced. He didn't know what lay ahead, but he was ready to face it. Whatever came next, he would approach it with the wisdom of someone who had walked through time and returned forever changed.

As he and Lila joined the townspeople, laughing and celebrating under the twinkling stars, Ethan knew one thing for certain: The adventure might have ended, but his journey—his true journey—had only just begun.

The End